Also by Randall Silvis

Narrative Non-Fiction

*Heart So Hungry: A Women's Extraordinary
Journey into the Labrador Wilderness,*
Knopf Canada, 2004
(Republished in the U.S. as *North of Unknown: Mina
Hubbard's Extraordinary Expedition into the Wilderness,*
Lyons Press, 2005)

Fiction

Disquiet Heart,
Thomas Dunne Books/St. Martin's Minotaur, 2002

On Night's Shore,
Thomas Dunne Books/St. Martin's Minotaur, 2001

Mysticus,
Wolfhawk Books, 1999

Dead Man Falling,
Carrol & Graf, 1997

Under the Rainbow,
Permanent Press, 1993

An Occassional Hell,
Permanent Press, 1993

Excelsior,
Henry Holt, 1987

The Luckiest Man in the World,
University of Pittsburgh Press, 1984

In a Town Called Mundomuerto

In a Town Called Mundomuerto

Randall Silvis

OMNIDAWN
RICHMOND, CALIFORNIA
2007

Cover Art: *An Angler* Artist: Tarsila do Amaral,
Medium: Oil on canvas.   Size: 66x75 cm.
Courtesy of The State Hermitage Museum, St. Petersburg, Russia

Book cover and interior design by Ken Keegan

Offset printed in the United States on archival, acid-free recycled paper
by Thomson-Shore, Inc., Dexter, Michigan

This is a work of fiction and all characters and events are fictitious.

**green
press**
INITIATIVE

Omnidawn Publishing is committed to preserving ancient
forests and natural resources. We elected to print *In A Town
Called Mundomuerto* on 50% post consumer recycled paper,
processed chlorine free. As a result, for this printing, we have
saved:

12 Trees (40' tall and 6-8" diameter)
4,893 Gallons of Wastewater
1,968 Kilowatt Hours of Electricity
539 Pounds of Solid Waste
1,060 Pounds of Greenhouse Gases

Omnidawn Publishing made this paper choice because our
printer, Thomson-Shore, Inc., is a member of Green Press
Initiative, a nonprofit program dedicated to supporting authors,
publishers, and suppliers in their efforts to reduce their use of
fiber obtained from endangered forests.

For more information, visit www.greenpressinitiative.org

Library of Congress Catalog-in-Publication Data
Silvis, Randall, 1950-
  In a town called Mundomuerto / Randall Silvis.
    p. cm.
  ISBN 978-1-890650-19-3 (pbk. : acid-free paper) --
  ISBN 978-1-890650-21-6 (acid free paper)
  1. Storytelling--Fiction. 2. Villages--Fiction.
  3. Reminiscing in old age--Fiction. 4. Superstition--Fiction. I. Title.
  PS3569.I4723515 2007
  813'.54--dc22
                                      2007007069

Published by Omnidawn Publishing
Richmond, California   www.omnidawn.com   (800) 792-4957

10 9 8 7 6 5 4 3 2 1

Softcover ISBN: 978-1-890650-19-3
Signed Limited 1st Edition of 500 Hardcover ISBN: 978-1-890650-21-6

Acknowledgements

The first part of this novel through to the last line on page 34 first appeared as the story "The Night of Love's Last Dance" in the anthology *ParaSpheres: Extending Beyond the Spheres of Literary and Genre Fiction — Fabulist and New Wave Fabulist Stories* (www.paraspheres.com), published by Omnidawn Publishing, 2006.

for Bret and Nathan
the magic of my life

In a Town Called Mundomuerto

In a town called Mundomuerto there lives a woman who bore a dolphin's child. She is an old woman now, la vieja, and most of the villagers dare glance at her only when she is looking the other way. But this is never difficult for she is always looking the other way, out to sea, where she watches for silvery fins to flash across the horizon like distant signal flags. Whether standing on the cliff's edge or on the rocky shore below, the vieja waits there for one of the flags to turn ashore ... for a handsome man dressed all in white to climb toward her over the patient rocks, his clothes miraculously dry by the time he reaches her, his fingertips kissing hers, "Will you dance with me, Lucia Luna?" A tall and graceful man with hips that move like water, his smile thin but sweet, his arm hooked around her back now, fingers caressing quivers into her spine, his left hand always atop his porkpie hat...

These days it is hard to believe that Lucia Luna was once a beauty. Her skin is darkly layered with years now, wrinkled with bitterness. Her hair is a tattered thundercloud that often wraps itself around the crag of her face. But there was a time, the grandfather says, when no man in town could keep his heart from dreaming of her.

The town was called Mundosuave then, and rightfully so, for in those days it was a tender place, a small village on a wide escarpment overlooking a generous sea ... a tiny world where, with hard work and kindness, life could be pleasant. But there is no one left to remember that time, there is only the grandfather and Lucia Luna herself. And because Lucia Luna will answer no questions except with a curse, a quick laceration of her jagged black eyes, it is left to the grandfather to tell the story. He tells it often, to anyone who will listen.

Now, after so many years, only the boy comes to request the story of how things came to be as they are. Each day the boy asks to hear the story again, because each time the tale unravels he catches a new thread of it or sees a new crease unfolding in the fabric. It is not a complicated story but as simple as the lives of the people who lived it, yet it holds a fascination for him, not unlike the fascination a child might feel when, with fear and curiosity, he tiptoes alone through the house of a stranger.

Still, the boy is fifteen now and there is not much child left in him. Some day he will not show up in the village square to ask for the grandfather's story, and on that day the boy in him will be gone and maybe the story gone with it. This is what the grandfather fears.

The grandfather's name, already forgotten in Mundomuerto, uttered now only by the tongues of his memory, had been Alberto when he was a boy. Years later he lost that name somehow, lost it like a handkerchief that falls from your pocket as you run too fast down an unmarked path. When you lose something in that manner you might try to retrieve it afterward but if you are not too dull you waste little time in this hopeless effort, you go on with your life nameless, trying on this name or that, but never again as certain of who you are as when you were young.

Were it not for his story and the boy who comes to listen, the old man would be as much a shadow as Lucia Luna as she passes unnoticed through the villagers' lives. But he is the grandfather for a while more at least, and in the late afternoon he sits on a broken chair in a corner of the clay-tiled square, gazing beyond the low stone wall that protects the plaza and its ghosts from tumbling into the sea. He sits in the gnarled shade of an acacia tree, a shade swept these days by nothing but the wind. Across his lap lays an old guitar, the veneer clouded and cracked, three strings missing. Behind him, the jungle has snaked its vines and branches onto the edge of the plaza, an encroachment which, like the dust and litter, goes unnoticed except by the grandfather, who likes to think that one of these days a vine will wrap itself around his ankles, and drag him, broken chair, tuneless guitar and all, back to that damp and shimmering place to which magic has retreated.

For now, the boy sits beside him on the dusty tiles. He too sits facing the ocean, though from his lower perspective he can see nothing but the most distant shimmering line against the burned-out blue of sky. The old man cannot see the shoreline either but his memory sees it clearly, the boulder in shallow water to which Lucia Luna would wade as the men returned home each night in their small boats, the boats riding low in the water, heavy with fish, Lucia Luna then seated atop the rock in her white dress with her strong brown legs widespread, feet bare, the hem of her dress pushed down between brown thighs.

"There was a time," the boy says, because the old man is not as quick with beginnings as he used to be, not as adept at walking with one foot in then and the other in now, "when Lucia Luna's smile was as warm as a night in August, as bright with promise as a Sunday's dawn."

The grandfather stares hard at the watery horizon glinting like metal, a fiery sun sinking toward it. He knows that below them, on the beach, an old woman in dirty rags is struggling toward a boulder.

The boy reaches up and softly plucks a guitar string. "Lucia Luna was seventeen that year," he says. "And you were fifteen, Grandfather. The same age as I am now."

After a moment, the old man looks down at him. "Surely you're not fifteen already. You were only twelve the last time I told you this—"

Without warning his words are swallowed by the throbbing boom of a helicopter as it comes roaring over the jungle, over the plaza and then tilting wildly to disappear down the coastline. The old man and the boy lower their heads and close their eyes against the whirl of dust these green and brown-mottled helicopters make. Outside the plaza a few chickens squawk and flutter for cover. A dog barks and chases the whirring bird, as ugly as a turkey vulture. A few moments later the dog turns and trots backs and flops against the nearest house.

The old man waits until the engine throb is no louder than a heartbeat. Then he says, "You can't be fifteen already, nieto. You were only twelve the last time I told this story."

"The last time was yesterday."

"The world moves fast these days, doesn't it? It's leaving me behind."

The boy remembers when he did not have to coax the story from the old man, when all the boy had to do was to try to keep up with it. "In the days of Mundosuave," he says, his voice little more than a whisper, "no man could look at Lucia Luna without feeling the slow heaviness of her breasts in his own blood, is that right?"

The old man has been looking at his sandals, his dusty feet. But now a smile deepens the creases in his face. "Los melones de dios," he says, and he lifts his head and he looks out across the sea. "She would come to the beach at dusk to sing for us as we brought in the day's catch. Someone would hand me my guitar the moment I hopped off my father's boat, and I would sit below her on the rock..."

As the old man talks the boy gazes into his red-rimmed eyes. There, as on the still surface of a tide pool, he looks for the image of a young Lucia Luna standing atop the boulder, stretching her arms and spine, tossing back her mane of raven hair. "She was like something wild, more animal than human," the old man says. "Can you see her, muchacho?"

The boy has found her now in the old man's eyes. "Yes, Grandfather."

"She's there?"

"Sí. You have her now."

The old man nods. For him, she is always there. "She would sit on the rock at dusk and sing to the ocean. All of Mundosuave would be gathered on the shore, unloading the boats and cleaning the fish. And all the young men would gaze up at her as she sang, their hearts throbbing nakedly."

"But only you," the boy says, "could get close to her. You would sit at her feet and play your guitar."

"I could feel her pulse in the strings of my guitar, nieto. Each time I plucked a string, I was touching her. And she... she felt my hands on her, I could see it in her eyes, and in the smile she sometimes turned on me."

"And at night," the boy says, "when the singing would end..."

"Her voice would sail off into the redness of the sky, and her body would shudder as if with pleasure, and I would lay my hands across the strings to quiet their trembling. And with my eyes closed I could feel Lucia Luna quivering from the sureness of my touch."

The boy glances quickly around the plaza, but no one is watching or listening. He is always embarrassed when the grandfather speaks of such things, yet he is fifteen and anxious to hear of them, for he too feels a whispering inside his chest as the story does things to him that he wishes to keep private.

"Except for the dolphin-man," the grandfather says, "I am the only man alive who ever made love to Lucia Luna. And I have never laid a finger on her..."

"In those days," the old man remembers, "we were still very much isolated from the world, and therefore older in many regards, with older ways of doing things. Men and women went about their business without stirring up a lot of dust, just as they had the day before and just as they expected to tomorrow. Seldom did anyone plan what he or she would do; one just did it, because the heart said *laugh,* the feet said *run,* or the belly said *eat.*

"The missionaries had been passing through Mundosuave for over a hundred years, leaving us Bibles and statues and trying to open our eyes to our debasement. But we were all slow learners, I guess. It took us a long time to realize that God was an angry old man in the clouds. In our simplicity we thought God was everywhere, in the ocean and the jungle, in the rocks, and yes, in the pretty statues of Mary and baby Jesus as well as in our dreams and our pants and even in our tortillas.

"There was a spirit to life in Mundosuave then, a trust, una esperanza. But this spirit... think of it, nieto, as a beautiful woman whose lover either neglects her or who sees her every smile as a flirtation with strangers, every sidelong glance as a betrayal, and who continually accuses her of deceit, and imprisons her, locks her in the house, never lets her beauty shine... Such a woman has no choice, I'm afraid, but to walk away into the sunset in search of a more tranquil home."

The old man, dissatisfied with his description of things, purses his lips and frowns. In all the tellings of his story, he has never yet felt he has gotten it right. And so he continues.

"It's hard to say what finally changed us. Maybe all that stuff from the missionaries finally sank in. I don't think we were changed by what happened to Lucia Luna, but the other way around. Her fate would not have played itself out as it did had we not already started down that twisted path of change."

It was in the late spring, he says, the end of the day, an evening of soft yellow light with clouds as pink as flamingoes. As the fishermen hauled their boats ashore, one of the waiting women, a fisherman's wife named Valencia Didión, always the first and last woman to speak, called out, "Another good day?"

Her husband answered, "They are all good days!"

Atop the wide round boulder which even at high tide protruded from the sea, Lucia Luna stood and stretched her arms to the sky, and every man who could risk it stole a glance at her as she rose onto her toes. Her skin was brown and her dress white and her hair and eyes as black and shiny as desire. "What song do you want to hear first?" she asked, her voice a melody in itself. Some of the men, when Lucia Luna spoke, were reminded of the pan flutes that are played by the Indians of the mountains far to the south; others thought they heard their mothers crooning lullabies; still others heard the harmony of the wind and sea calling out of sight of the land.

Jorge Canales, a man who was built like a barrel with four stubby limbs, said, "A song of love, what else? Sing about how you dream of me each night, bella."

"Hurry up, Alberto," the grandfather's mother teased as he, still just a boy, hopped out of his father's boat. She handed him his guitar and said, "Play something quick, before Jorge's imagination tells him another lie."

Fifteen-year-old Alberto, bare-chested and grinning, splashed toward the boulder. Careful not to get his guitar wet, he sat on the edge of the boulder and looked up at Lucia Luna. When she sat too, spreading her feet for balance and pushing the dress down between her thighs, his eyes were level with the calves of her naked legs.

"She needed only to look at me," the grandfather says, "and I knew what song she wanted me to play."

With the first chord Alberto strummed, the villagers fell silent. They worked with smiles, their hands finding the rhythms of Lucia's songs, first a ballad of impossible and tragic romance, then a comic tale about a man whose wife is so lazy that he trades her for a goat that can cook, then another tragic song about a fisherman who drowns himself in search of a mermaid.

Alberto, as he played, caressed the neck and strings of his guitar as if he were caressing Lucia Luna herself, his left hand around the curve of her ankle, right hand strumming the inside of her thigh. With each song his hands became bolder, until he was holding her so hard against him that he could not tell where his throbbing ended and hers began.

"Good job, Alberto," one of the men told him at the end of the third song. "You got almost half the chords right that time."

Lucia reached down to tousle the boy's hair. "Don't pay any attention to him. You're getting better all the time."

"It's because your beautiful voice tells my fingers what to do," he said, so softly that even she did not appear to hear.

"Let's have another one, chica," someone called from the beach. "Something snappier this time."

But Lucia Luna placed her hands on her knees and stood atop the boulder. "That's enough for now," she said. "Tonight at fiesta I will sing every song I know."

"And I will play for only you," Alberto whispered.

But she did not even look at him. She was standing with hands on her hips and looking instead at Jorge Canales, who had announced that Lucia Luna would dance her first dance with him tonight.

"Only if you wash the smell of fish off you first," she said.

Jorge turned to the man working beside him, jabbed him in the ribs and said, "Some of us like the smell of fish, eh Pablo?"

Pablo said, "Personally, I would rather eat it than smell it."

The other men hooted at this while the women, trying to hide their smiles, clicked their tongues and shook their heads. A woman who was nearly as round as Jorge Canales told him, "Maybe both of you should bring a tuna to the party tonight."

Jorge answered, "If you'll bring *your* tuna, I will bring my sperm whale."

She picked out a fish no bigger than her little finger and threw it at him. "Here's your whale, you dreamer!"

At this even the women laughed openly, especially when Jorge picked up the tiny fish and dangled it near his crotch, as if comparing the fish to his manhood. He pouted for a moment, wounded by the woman's insult. Then his eyes brightened. Holding the fish's tail against his crotch he ran after the woman, the little fish flopping between his legs. She screamed and ran a few steps this way, then turned heavily and fled in the other direction, Jorge bellowing like a whale as he chased after her.

"Stop running, you two," somebody scolded. "You are making the ground shake."

Only Alberto did not join in the laughter. His eyes never left Lucia Luna.

≈≈≈

That night, after the boatloads of sardines had been laid out to dry, there was a fiesta in honor of one of the many

holidays which the people of Mundomuerto no longer cel-
ebrate. The square in the center of town was swept clean
and set ablaze with torches. Along the stone wall sat tables
heavy with roasted meats and fish, tall stacks of tortillas,
earthen bowls of red and green picantes, gourds filled with
pulque and pitchers brimming with red wine. For the children there were candied fruits and glazed sweets.

Young Alberto and three of his friends stood on a small
platform and provided the music. They sang as well as
played, and if they were not good musicians they were good
fishermen who happened to own instruments and this was
as much as anyone expected. The tempo was always bright
and the dust raised by stomping feet was never too thick, it
sparkled in the colored lights, as soothing a dance floor as
crushed velvet.

Lucia Luna was seventeen that year, as full and ripe a
woman as any man could envision. Flowing from the arms
of one partner into those of another, she allowed each man
a single dance, starting with the youngest because they had
neither patience nor endurance, only the desire to stand
close to her as soon as possible. Each man when dismissed
would stagger back to the tables lined against the stone wall,
needing to clear his head with something less intoxicating
than the scent and heat of Lucia Luna. Then, knowing that
his moment of grace had come and gone, he would take
one of the plainer girls into his arms—they were all plain
girls compared to Lucia Luna—and expiate his hunger in a
more appreciative embrace.

The older men bided their time, waiting for their wives
to grow sleepy with too much food or wine or indifference.
Then each of these men in turn would sneak into Lucia
Luna's arms, hoping to catch her off guard long enough
that he might pull her close and feel the hardness of a breast
stabbing his heart, and perhaps then to press his own hard-

ness against her, inflame her, maybe to drop his hand onto her buttock for one discreet squeeze of that heavenly muscle.

Lucia Luna, however, held each of her partners at a distance. In her arms each man occupied a position two feet short of intimacy. She would allow a partner close enough that he might be dizzied by the musky warmth that radiated from her, but never near enough that he could honestly claim to have felt the breeze of her laughter upon his neck, or to have truly known that delicious fatality of feeling the knife tips of her breasts carve initials into his heart.

Every man, when he wandered away from her, his arms profoundly empty, thought to himself something like *I failed to touch her soul,* and he spent the rest of the night trying to numb his misery. What only a few of the men realized—and those who did sensed it only as a wordless suspicion—was that Lucia Luna longed to have her soul touched by a man. In fact she wanted it as desperately as each of her partners wanted to give her that frightening joy.

To the other young women her laughter and whirling dress marked her as frivolous, all flesh and ego. But on occasion, between dances, in that murmuring stillness when the only music is the sound of insects flying at the torches, Lucia Luna's smile would falter, her gaze would wander to the stars or the jungle or across the open sea, and those villagers able to perceive it would guess that there was more to Lucia Luna than mere beauty, there was the sadness of those who, through no fault of their own, want too much and, because they have never yet achieved their extravagant desire, cannot even name it.

All evening long the young Alberto watched her from his vantage point on the bandstand. Through the haze of dust and the speckled clouds of gnats he followed her every step. He felt, from the very first note, that he was playing for only her, and each time another man took Lucia Luna into his arms, Alberto felt that man's feet dancing on his shadow, trampling his swollen heart.

Once, when he plucked a guitar string in a certain way and its single high note reverberated like a shrill moan through the heavy air, Lucia spun in her partner's arms to stare at Alberto, her mouth slightly open as if she needed to pant for the next breath, her black eyes alive with golden sparks.

"When she turned and looked at me like that," the grandfather says, "my insides went hollow. I knew then that my misery had touched her in just the right place, a place of its own knowing. It was all I could do to keep from stumbling backward off the platform and falling unconscious into the bushes."

He managed, however, to play on, strumming only a few errant chords until he caught up with the other musicians again.

Lucia Luna licked her lips and grinned at him. Alberto went empty with everything but desire, and he knew in his heart that he existed only for this evening, to lie with her later that same night, to be her first and ever lover. He knew from her smile that now she understood this too.

And so, for the next hour, Alberto played in sweet delirium. His hardness throbbed against the back of the guitar. It grew harder, he imagined, with each chord he strummed, stretching like a tree root growing toward water. "The only thing that worried me," the grandfather says, "was the tremendous pressure I felt inside. I was afraid that when Lucia and I finally made love, the explosion might do her some damage."

The old man grins at the boy. "Have you ever felt that way yourself, muchacho? Do you feel the cannonball wanting to explode?"

The boy's face goes hot, and he looks away. He sits very still, hands clasped in his lap. "Perhaps we should continue with the story now."

The grandfather laughs softly and nods.

The merrymaking proceeded long into the night, he tells the boy. Lucia Luna exhausted one partner after another, each man enervated by his single dance with her. But as the men's faces paled with exhaustion, Lucia Luna's cheeks glowed. Some who watched imagined that she absorbed the men's energies. A few of the older folks thought they detected in her wild swirls an urgency, a desperation. In any case even the musicians soon drooped, each eventually laying down his instrument to make his way to a long table beneath a cieba tree, where he sought fortification in the tapas and wine.

"Only I remained on the stand," the grandfather says, "my left hand fingering the chords of her desire, my right hand stroking her resonating soul." Lucia Luna danced alone in the beaten dust, her only partner the sighing moonlight. "Her white dress billowed about her legs while her feet trod the heartbeat of the earth. And her scent! Even on the bandstand it came to me. At one point I saw it rather than smelled it. Her fragrance swarmed over me like a cloud of fireflies, and then enveloped me, a million hot pinpricks of her scent. She must have seen it too, because that was when she danced over close to me and faced me as she danced. Her smile was so luminous that it embarrassed even the torches. One by one I heard them sputtering out."

In silence the whole town watched. Slouched in their chairs or slunk against the stone wall, they made no move to stumble home. Alberto played song after song, and Lucia Luna sang more sweetly than ever.

"What only I realized," the grandfather says, "was that she was not merely singing, she was giving voice to ecstasy.

Her luxurious gyrations were not mere dance, they were a response to my long root of ardor as it wormed its way inside her."

After a while, the grandfather says, he found it necessary to pause for a moment and catch his breath. Also, he felt that his lower body was about to detonate at any second. In fact when he looked down it seemed to be pulsating of its own volition. He attempted to conceal this activity behind his guitar, but then a loud knocking sound ensued, an especially curious sound—except to him—because his hands were perfectly motionless.

To keep from erupting in public, Alberto bowed once to Lucia Luna, then stepped discreetly off the rear of the platform and, after placing his guitar on the back of the bandstand, he melted into the darkness. He meant to return as soon as he had brought himself under control once more.

Lucia Luna softly laughed. Stretching and yawning she did a slow pirouette, one full turn so that she ended up facing the bandstand again. "It was at that moment," the grandfather says, "when the stranger appeared. No one could later say from which direction the man had come."

From out of the shadows he walked, a tall man, and thin, dressed, like Lucia Luna, all in white. He wore a linen suit, white shoes, and a collarless white shirt buttoned tight around his neck. Even his hat was white—a straw porkpie hat—but its band was bright yellow, as yellow as a rising moon. He walked with a carriage eminently erect without being rigid. His stride barely scuffed the earth. Some people later remarked that he moved like water; others said he was as fluid as an apparition.

In any case he was soon standing behind Lucia Luna. She must have felt his presence, for without turning she pulled her hair off the back of her neck and let it fall over her shoulder. For a moment it seemed he would lean forward and kiss the knob of her spine. Instead he reached up and touched his fingertips to her arm.

At his touch Lucia Luna turned, smiling. And in that instant when she beheld him, his thin sweet smile, she gasped. This in itself was extraordinary—that the mere sight of a man, any man, could elicit such a response from her. Always before, it had been the men who gasped.

Alberto peered out from the darkness behind the bandstand. To his eyes the stranger was good-looking, yes, but not exceptional. His face was thin and his skin rough, maybe even pockmarked, though it was difficult to ascertain this by the meager light. Still, Alberto saw no reason why Lucia Luna should suddenly be trembling, or why she should assume such a submissive posture, her left arm laid across the small of her back, the middle fingertip of her right hand resting in the hollow of her throat.

With his own left hand the stranger held lightly to the brim of his hat, as if the wind might blow it away, though the night was still. He extended his right hand and touched his fingertips to hers. "Will you dance with me, Lucia Luna?"

Even the insects seemed to hush before his words. Then there was only the sound of waves on the rocky shore below, the crash of surf and then its sigh of capitulation. Lucia Luna said, her voice as small as a fledgling, "There is no music, señor."

At this the stranger turned to the three musicians sprawled beneath a cieba tree. He smiled upon them as if they were all old friends, as if they had been babies in the same crib. "Compadres," he said, "por favor? A night like this, without your music, is like a sky without the moon or stars."

Without a word to one another the musicians stumbled to their feet, returned smiling to their instruments, and began to play. Lucia Luna moved into the stranger's arms—or, more accurately, into his arm, for his left hand never strayed far from the brim of his porkpie hat. But even with only one arm he managed to hold her closer than had any man before him. Their gazes locked. The stranger's hand lay flat between her shoulder blades, his skin a shade paler than her own, Lucia Luna's breasts crushed against his chest.

Alberto, crouching in pain in the bushes, felt a new pain shoot into his chest now, as if a jagged thread on a thick needle had been pushed down through his heart.

"How is it that you know my name?" he heard Lucia Luna inquire of the stranger.

"I have been hearing your name my entire life," the man said.

"From who?"

"From every bird that ever sang, hermosa. From every breeze that scrapes the sky."

"I never realized I was so famous," she teased.

"Even the ocean whispers your name. Can't you hear it? *Lucia Luna! Lucia Luna! Lucia Luna!*"

She made a slight turn then, fitting a hip between his legs. "Why don't you put your other arm around me too?" she asked.

"Because the joy of holding you in both arms would be too much for me to bear." Now and then as the couple danced, Alberto closed his eyes, hoping to erase this scene off the face of the night. But each time he peered out through the jewels of moisture shimmering on his eyelashes, there they were again, as beautiful and terrifying as a fever dream.

Valencia Didión had been squinting at the stranger ever since he arrived. The mother of three boys, the youngest a year older than Alberto, she had spent much of her life with her face screwed-up in a critical squint. For this fiesta she and her husband had sat side by side all night long in the cane chairs they dragged from their house. They had danced not a single dance—though her husband was, at that moment, swaying to the rhythm of his own snores, his arms filled with an ethereal Lucia Luna.

Valencia jabbed a very real elbow into his ribs. He sat upright and blinked. "Who is that man?" she hissed into his ear.

Señor Didión needed a few moments to adjust to consciousness. Then he answered, "Ask him, not me." A few seconds later he added, "That hat he wears looks like a little bucket for catching sardines."

"Maybe it is," Valencia said.

"Is that supposed to mean something?"

"Shhh," she said. "Be quiet and let me study him a while."

Alberto, too, had been studying the stranger. "And the more I studied him," the grandfather remembers, "the more that ache in my testicles throbbed. It ceased to be the ache of love and became instead the hot red ache of having been kicked there. I felt too sore to walk, but I crawled to my feet anyway, and I managed to cross the plaza to him. It was like walking through a long dark tunnel, with only the glow of Lucia Luna's smoldering eyes to light my way."

Three times Alberto tapped on the stranger's shoulder, attempting to cut in. But he might as well have been tapping on air. Finally he grasped Lucia Luna's wrist and pulled it off the stranger's waist. "Alberto, please," Lucia Luna said, and barely bothered to look at him. "This gentleman and I are dancing."

"But I want to dance with you now."

"Later, chico."

"I've been playing for you all night. It's my turn to dance!"

"Then go find yourself a little girl to dance with, hermanito."

Alberto stood there rigid with anger. Although the whole world had gone black for him, he could feel the grins of the villagers. Their chuckles were like mosquitoes to him, their whispers like snakes.

Lucia Luna was already oblivious to his presence. "Have we ever met before?" she asked the stranger.

"A thousand times at least," he said.

"And where would that have been?"

"In my dreams, mariposa."

She lay her head upon his shoulder. "That explains why you look so familiar."

Alberto reeled away from them, breathless, one hand feeling for the knife that had been thrust into his heart. Even as he staggered out of the plaza he wondered what evil powers kept him upright when all he wanted was insentience, and how it was possible to keep walking with nothing but a black hole where your heart had been, and why God, so obviously malicious, did not now rush in at Alberto's repeated invitation and finish the young man off.

———

It was not until morning, when Alberto came wandering back into the square—

"What about where you spent the night?" the boy interrupts.

The grandfather asks, "What about it?"

"You left out the part about where you spent the night."

The old man thinks for a moment. He can see a fog-bank of gray, he can hear water spilling onto rocks, but that is all. "I've decided that it isn't important," he says. "It slows the story down."

"It has always seemed important to me."

"When you are a boy, everything is important. But when you are an old man, almost nothing is."

"What you did that night," the boy says, unwilling to let this hole in the story go unfilled, "is you just kept walking until your legs gave out on you. It was only then you realized that you were lying on the beach a mile from town. That's when the thought occurred to you that if you walked into the ocean and drowned ..."

The old man nods mournfully. "The tide might wash my body ashore where the fishermen would find it in the morning."

"You knew that the sight of your body would pitch the entire village into sorrow."

"And what remorse and guilt would seize Lucia Luna herself."

"So you got up and you dragged yourself into the water. Out to where the moon lay like a golden doily on the sea."

"Here comes the part you wouldn't let me forget," the old man says.

"But not even the ocean would have you. It spit you back onto the rocks, and slapped you so hard that a kick from a horse would have been more pleasant."

"You're a cruel boy for one so young," the old man tells him.

"And so you lay there all night, neither awake nor asleep. The fog rolled in and tried to smother you, and you wished it success."

"But too much pain immunizes a man from death," the old man continues. "So finally the fog gave up and called it quits. Then a red-winged blackbird came and—"

"I thought it was a parrot," the boy says.

"Who was it saw this bird, you or me?"

"Yesterday it was a parrot, Grandfather."

"Then it must have been wearing a disguise, because today it is a blackbird. Take it or leave it."

"All right," says the boy. "A red-winged blackbird came and perched beside your head."

"And all night long it laughed at me in a woman's voice."

"Lucia Luna's."

"Of course Lucia Luna's. And its breath smelled like the fog. And its laughter was distant and muffled, as if it came from deep down the blackbird's throat, which is what happens when a bird pecks out your memory and gobbles it down. I kept reaching for that bird, thinking I would wring its neck and shake my memory loose, but after a couple of tries I couldn't lift my arm anymore and I just said 'The hell with it, take it. Just make sure you get it all. Don't leave a speck of it behind to haunt me.'"

The old man pauses now. He looks down at the face of his battered guitar.

The boy says, perhaps because he is feeling guilty for wounding the old man with this memory, "It is a significant part of the story, just as I thought."

"Now that I've heard it again," the old man answers, "I am less certain of that than ever."

It was not until morning, when Alberto wandered back into the square—coming, as might a dazed accident victim, to gaze upon the debris of his misfortune and to search the rubble for reason—and there overheard the women talking as they gathered up the cups and bowls and swept the plaza clean, that he began to understand what had transpired in his absence.

"... but to leave with him after just one dance," Valencia Didión was saying as Alberto retrieved his guitar from the bandstand. "That alone should tell you what kind of woman she is."

There were eight other women helping to clean the plaza, and many of them nodded in agreement. But Rosario Morales said, "They danced two dances at least." She picked up a plate with a small lizard stuck on it, his front legs encased in a pool of hardened caramel sauce. "I watched them with my own eyes." She held the plate upside down to see how long the lizard would dangle there before it fell.

"I counted six dances," a third woman said.

"If you want to call it dancing," said Valencia Didión, "fine. But it looked like something else to me."

The lizard hung by only one leg now. Its long tail batted back and forth, snapping against the plate. "Even so, we must remember that a visit from a dolphin-man is a blessing."

"To dance with a dolphin-man is a blessing," said Valencia. "But to sneak off with him into the darkness ..." She snorted as if she had inhaled a bug, then swatted her broom at the plaza tiles. At the same moment, the lizard dropped from Rosario Morales's plate. In a flash it scampered up and over the stone wall and flung itself into freedom.

Alberto, who had been lingering near the side of the bandstand, pretending to be concerned with nothing but the dew on the lacquered face of his guitar, could not stop himself from asking, "Do you really think he was a dolphin-man?"

Moments earlier his husk of misery had split open to reveal a flower of hope, a tight bud ready to bloom. For if the stranger was indeed a dolphin-man, that would explain everything. It would explain the effect he had had on Lucia Luna, her entrancement with his pale smile. Moreover, if this was the case, Alberto had been bested not by a mere human, but by a demigod in a linen suit, an angel of the sea. Alberto found himself smiling. No wonder Lucia Luna had spurned him. All night long he had caressed her with his music, had even eased inside her with his every thought, and then, at just the right moment, along came a shape-changer to steal her with his magic. Lucia Luna, in such a situation, must be held blameless. Suddenly Alberto's chest did not feel crushed by an anchor.

"Why aren't you out with the others?" Valencia asked.

Alberto stepped forward. "Did the stranger admit to being a dolphin-man?"

"Did you see his hat or didn't you?"

Rosario Morales giggled. "Alberto had his moon-eyes on all night. And there is only one thing a man wearing moon-eyes can see."

"Two," said another woman, "when they are as big as Lucia Luna's."

All the women laughed, all except Valencia Didión.

It is at this point in the old man's story, as he pauses to take a breath, which he often forgets to do, that the boy interrupts. "I have always wondered," the boy says, "why Valencia Didión was such an unpleasant person."

"You've never seen unhappiness?" the grandfather asks. "You, a boy living alone with a mother who screams at him from morning through night?"

"But this was in Mundosuave, not here."

"Same place, different day."

"Even so, it must have been a paradise compared to this. You've said so yourself. It makes it hard to understand why Valencia Didión, especially now, before everything happens, couldn't have been a little nicer."

The old man shrugs and runs a callused hand over the guitar strings. "Every story needs a villain," he says.

"Sometimes I think the dolphin-man is the villain. And then later, that the villain must be Poco the Giant. And then your father, and Señor Luna too."

"In stories as in life," the old man says, "there is never any shortage of villains."

"It's only near the end when I begin to think there are no villains at all."

"Don't get ahead of me," the old man tells him. "It throws me off the track."

"I'm just trying to understand her better. Because of the way the story makes me feel about her later."

"Who, Valencia Didión? She was born that way probably; born with a sour taste in her mouth. Or maybe she grew into it. Nothing ever satisfied her, that's all there was to it. You either accept it or you don't."

"I'm very happy to accept it," the boy says. "But I would like to understand it too."

"Take a look around, nieto. Do you understand any of this?"

The boy looks at the dusty plaza, wide sections of the stone wall in ruins. Through a gaping hole to his right he can view trampled yards littered with broken plastic toys, empty plastic bottles, beer cans and chunks of plastic foam and all manner of objects recovered from the beach by children who drag them up to the escarpment only to soon discard them again. Sometimes the wind blows them back over the cliff for another child to find and drag up the narrow path.

The boy stares at all this for so long that his mind goes blank. When he turns to the grandfather again, he has forgotten whether he is listening to yesterday's version or today's. "Where were we in the story?" he asks.

"We left Alberto staring blankly at Valencia Didión. Then he asked her, 'What difference does a hat make?'"

"Did you see him take it off?" the woman countered. "Even once? No, you did not. Because all night long he held his hat in place."

Still Alberto did not understand.

"To cover up his blowhole!" Valencia shouted at him.

"All I know," said a woman to a withered vieja working nearby, "is that it's about time it happened to Mundosuave. I remember how my grandmother used to talk about—"

"It is our turn, es verdad. Cuechaca and Nuevas Alijas have each been visited twice so far."

"It's been three times for Mochillo!"

"Maybe if he liked it here he'll come back."

"Our problem is that we don't have enough fiestas."

"Or enough pretty girls maybe. The dolphins only turn themselves into men so as to dance with the prettiest girls."

"Thank God for Lucia Luna."

"You'd better hope you are thanking the right person," said Valencia Didión. She made the sign of the cross, then returned to her sweeping.

"It will bring good luck to the entire village," a woman told her. "You'll see."

"To dance with a dolphin-man is good luck," Valencia repeated. "To *dance.* The other ... The other is an abomination."

"It couldn't have been all that bad," another woman said. "Rosario peeked in Lucia Luna's window a few minutes ago, and there she was still sleeping like a baby."

"With a smile a foot long on her face," said Rosario.

"A foot long would make me smile too," another woman said.

Some of the women laughed so hard that they had to sit down a while. Valencia Didión, however, continued to sweep the tiles, stirring up more dust with her broom straws than a full night of dancing had done.

And so Alberto, with his adolescent pride assuaged but his grief redoubled at the thought of another man, even a magical one, doing those things to Lucia Luna that destiny had reserved for him, trudged home long enough to put his guitar safely away. His mother handed him a warm tortilla with a few pieces of chicken meat inside and warned him not to keep his father waiting. Alberto nodded without having heard anything she said, and he wandered toward the cliff path. Along the way he tossed his breakfast to a fat dog that grinned at him from the shade of a house.

With joy and misery taking turns punching him from the inside out, Alberto stumbled down the narrow cliff path. Most of the boats had already set off, their captains poling carefully into open water, toward those places where the activity of birds or the shadows of the sea would tell them to throw their nets. Alberto's father's boat was the last to depart. It floated ten yards from shore, Alberto's father knee-deep in the surf as he pushed his skiff to sea. He was just about to climb aboard when he noticed his son wandering down the beach, head bowed, shoulders drooping.

"Hurry up if you're coming!" he called to the boy.

At this Alberto turned and looked. The expression on his face suggested that he had no idea who his father was, or what he was doing out there. "Andale!" his father called. "You think the fish are going to come to us?"

Alberto walked a bit more quickly now. It had occurred to him that it would be good to have something to do for a while, something other than pulling himself to his feet just so he could knock himself back down. He climbed into the small boat and took his position forward, facing the horizon with the carefully folded net at his feet. His father sat at the stern and rowed them toward the purple shadow of a reef.

Alberto sat with his back hunched. When he spoke, he felt a chill on his neck. "Some of the women are saying that the stranger last night was a dolphin-man."

His father rowed one stroke on his right side, then swung the oar to his left. Heavy drops of water struck Alberto's back. "Who knows?" his father said. "Women can't be wrong all the time."

"It would mean good things for the village, wouldn't it?"

His father did not respond to this. He had just now noticed a thin line of gray creeping into the morning sky, like the first crack in a porcelain vase. He paddled without talking for several minutes, then finally said, "Keep your eyes on those clouds today."

The grandfather, in telling this story, stares at the horizon as if he too has spotted a thundercloud sneaking toward them. Then he pulls at the corners of his mouth and runs his tongue over his lips. "I could use something to drink," he says.

"You always say that," the boy reminds him. "And I always offer to get you something."

"And then how do I respond?"

"You say, 'It is easier to live with a thirst than to constantly try to quench it.'"

"I guess I must like to complain," the old man says.

The boy smiles. He waits for the story to continue. He is about to reach up and delicately pluck a string of the guitar when a pebble comes flying out of nowhere and strikes his arm. He swats at the place where he thinks he has been stung, and in so doing sees two other boys standing nearby, grinning.

Luis, the taller of the two boys, tells him, "There's a yacht full of gringos anchored up around the point. We're going to row out and see what they've got."

The old man can tell that the boy would like to join his friends, but he has never left in the middle of the story before. "Go with them," the grandfather says. "Go have some fun."

"It isn't fun for me to beg for favors."

"Then take some oranges to sell."

"The oranges aren't very good this year."

Ernesto, the other boy, speaks up. "The gringos don't care, they'll buy anything. The men are drinking beer and the women are lying on the deck with their tops off."

"Are you coming or not?" asks Luis.

"Go, nieto. It isn't good to spend all your time with such an old piece of wood as me."

The boy looks to his friends and tries to explain. "He was telling me about the dolphin-man."

Both Luis and Ernesto frown, their mouths twisting as if they want to spit out something sour.

The old man tells him, "Why sit here and listen to the story again. You know it by heart, you could tell it yourself."

Softly the boy answers, "But you're the one who lived it."

"Sometimes I wonder about that." A moment later he adds, "Go on. Go get something for yourself while you still can."

Almost sadly, the boy pushes himself to his feet, eyes on the ground. He takes one step toward his friends, then looks up at them. "I'll catch up with you in a minute," he says.

He waits until Ernesto and Luis have run off, then turns to the grandfather again. "There is something I thought of last week that I want to ask you about."

The old man raises his eyebrows slightly, he cocks his head.

"Other than Alberto," the boy says, "other than you yourself, there are no young people in your story. No children. Why is that?"

The old man looks surprised. "How strange that I never noticed it myself!"

"There must have been children in Mundosuave, weren't there?"

"There must have been, por supuesto."

"It makes me wonder why none of them ever show up in your story."

"They must have all run off somewhere," the grandfather says.

"Where would they have gone?"

For a moment the old man is as puzzled as the boy, but then he remembers something. He remembers a meadow between the jungle and the sea, a silvery waterfall splashing into a stream. And the old man smiles. "When you come back we will go on with the story, and maybe the answer will occur to us."

The boy nods solemnly. "I'll remember where we stopped."

"Luego," the grandfather says.

The boy shuffles away then, still held by the gravity of something he does not yet understand. A minute later he looks back at the old man, who has let his chin sink onto his chest and has closed his eyes. The boy smiles, turns and breaks into a run. "Wait for me!" he calls.

The old man looks up then and watches him go. Then he speaks to the broken face of his guitar. "The boy is right, the oranges are bad this year. They lost their sweetness a long time ago, didn't they?"

But it is a sweetness the old man can still taste, a dulce he savors by letting his eyes go unfocused and his sadness go slack. As he pushes himself up by degrees and shuffles toward the wall at the edge of the square, his gaze is turned inward. There he can see a half dozen women below him in the orange grove of his memory, their baskets and aprons bulging with fruit while he, like a hovering angel, lies across a heavy limb so as to lower the fruit to their hands.

Because of the threat of storm the fishermen came home early the day after the fiesta, but there had been no storm after all, only a rumbling grayness that dissipated in the late afternoon. Alberto wandered out to the orange grove to gaze on Lucia Luna, to see if she looked changed or bewitched or if she carried herself differently after her night with the stranger, but the women spotted him and sent him up into a tree as their apprentice. From that vantage point he could not only hear everything they said, he could fill his eyes with what he saw down the front of Lucia Luna's dress. In that instant he forgave her everything, every hurtful word and humiliation. His body grew so heavy with desire that the branch beneath him creaked.

"If he was just a peddler," he heard Valencia Didión saying from the other side of the tree, a direction he did not bother to look, "then where were his goods?"

"Sold," Lucia answered beneath him. Each time she moved to pick from another branch, Alberto moved too, her pet squirrel. "Everything had been sold."

"La boba," Valencia growled. "He sold *you* a bill of goods."

Lucia Luna only smiled.

"What I wonder," another woman said, "is why we've never seen him around here before. Mundosuave gets its share of peddlers, but never one like him."

"He's young," Lucia explained, "and just starting out. He's looking for new places to go."

"He found a new place last night, didn't he?"

"You women are like a bunch of blind chickens," Lucia told them. "You're pecking for corn but only hitting the stones."

Her denials whetted their curiosity even more.

Valencia asked, "How do you account for that silly-looking hat he never once removed?"

"It wasn't my hat nor my head, so why ask me?"

"I would have reached right up and plucked it off," a woman said.

"Maybe I did."

"And when this happened," said Valencia, "did he blow water or air?"

"When you open your mouth, amiga," Lucia countered, smiling sweetly, "do you blow anything besides bad breath?"

Several of the women laughed at this, but Valencia Didión glowered. Lucia Luna chose this instant to reach into her apron pocket and pull something out. Alberto saw only a flash of yellow, as lithe as a string of light. But Rosario Morales, who was standing nearest Lucia Luna, shrieked with amazement.

"My god, look at that bracelet!" In a moment she was rubbing it between her fingers, a delicate braid of metal as slender as a snake's tongue. "Is it real gold?" she asked.

Lucia Luna shrugged. "I didn't ask."

"Here, let me have a look," another woman said. Soon they were all huddled around Lucia Luna, each taking a turn holding the bracelet to the light or draping it over their own wrists.

"Where would a peddler get a bracelet like this?" one of them asked.

"More importantly, why would he give it to *you?*"

"You must have made him very happy, chica."

"I think it's only gold-plated. I had one just like it once, but I threw it away after my wrist turned green."

Lucia Luna reclaimed the bracelet and deftly fastened it in place. "I never wear green," she said. "So I'm not worried about that." She went back to picking oranges then, blithely indifferent to the covetous glances of her friends. Valencia Didión in particular could not keep her eyes off the bracelet.

"You're going to snag it on a branch," she warned. "A little thing like that will snap in half if you so much as look at it sideways."

"I like the way it catches the light."

A few minutes later Valencia Didión remarked, "What is it the Bible says? 'As a jewel of gold in a swine's snout, so is a fair woman which is without discretion.'"

To this Lucia Luna merely smiled and, reaching high for an orange, jiggled her arm.

Valencia Didión worked in bitter silence for a few minutes, plucking oranges as if she were pinching the heads off shrimp. Finally she could contain her resentment no longer. "A cheap trinket for a few minutes of pleasure," she scoffed. "I guess that's the going rate."

Lucia Luna shot back, "And I guess that explains why you wake up empty-handed every morning."

For a moment Valencia Didión neither moved nor spoke as she and Lucia Luna locked stares. To Rosario Morales

they resembled a pair of horned lizards, each ready to shoot
a stream of blood from her eyes. In the end it was the older
woman who turned away. She reached to her right and
yanked at an orange so hard that Alberto, who until then
had not realized she was picking from his branch, bounced
twice. "Move to another limb!" she scolded. "Can't you see
I've picked this one clean?"

But her voice was a distant howl to Alberto, so entranced was he with the brown vista of Lucia Luna's shoulders and breasts that most of the conversation had rustled
past him with little effect. All he realized was that Lucia
Luna was now looking up at him. She smiled, then jerked
her head toward the adjoining branch. Alberto scampered
onto it. "At least there's one person in town who will believe me," she said. And in that moment no town existed
for Alberto, there was only this small but perfect universe
in which he floated just above Lucia Luna's head.

"He's no different than any other man," Valencia
Didión said. "He'll believe anything his pimiento tells him
to believe."

At this the women laughed, grateful for a break in the
tension. One of them, he could not see who, reached up to
tickle him between the legs.

"Now look what you've done," said Lucia, pretending
not to be amused. "You've made him blush."

"Is your pimiento blushing too, Alberto?" somebody
asked. "Come down and let us see."

"Have you had your pimiento picked yet, chico?"

"He's letting it ripen for Lucia Luna, aren't you,
Alberto?"

"It needs to grow a little more, I think."

"I think it grows every time he looks at her."

"In that case, come on down here, Alberto. We'll use
your pimiento as a ladder."

Alberto buried his face in the sweet-smelling leaves. The women held their bellies and rocked with laughter. When he peeked down he saw Lucia Luna looking up at him and grinning. And when Lucia winked, Alberto felt all the breath explode from his lungs. His perch seemed to evaporate from beneath him and he tumbled off, thudding onto his back at Lucia's feet.

For just a moment the women started toward him, but then they saw the expression on his face, the glaze of his eyes and his feeble, moronic smile, and instead of coming to his aid they howled with laughter, some of them cackling so hard that they dropped the corners of their aprons, spilling oranges onto the ground.

Even Lucia Luna put a hand to her mouth and giggled. Rosario Morales stuffed a half dozen oranges into her own blouse, then stood over Alberto with her hips thrust back and her mountainous bosom blocking out the sun. "Ooh, pimiento grande!" she crooned. "Look out! look out! I think I'm going to explode for you!" With that she pulled out the tail of her shirt and let the oranges tumble down atop Alberto, plopping onto his chest as she wiggled and moaned lasciviously.

Alberto rolled his head this way and that to avoid the falling oranges, but without much success. And soon he was laughing too, the fruits' oils redolent in his nostrils, his face sticky with juice. Even as the laughter faded and the women returned to their work he lay there never wanting to leave, the sun through the branches a huge and brilliant orange, the soft thud of feet treading all around him, the occasional giggle as an orange was rolled between his legs. Only the black cloud of Valencia's face momentarily darkened his euphoria, but he looked quickly away from it, he lay his cheek to the cool earth and watched Lucia Luna as she picked, her firm brown hand plucking his heart again and again and again…

"It seemed, at that moment," the grandfather says to the clouds, "that nothing could ever go wrong with the world." He is standing at the low stone wall now, his gaze sliding down across the sky, coming inland, easing toward shore.

"It seemed, to the boy I was back then, that our illusion of happiness was a dream that need never end." Upside down on shore is half a fishing boat, a curve of splinters and jagged boards. On a boulder surrounded by water somebody has left a pile of black rags, a wind-tattered bundle of madness and hope in a shape vaguely suggesting a woman.

≈

For the next few days, nothing much changed. Lucia Luna clung tenaciously to her story about the stranger, that he was a peddler named Arcadio Martín from the port town of Nuevas Alijas nearly fifty miles to the south. Yes, she had wandered off to be alone with him after the fiesta, but only to get away from the probing eyes and fluttering tongues. And all night long he had chattered like a magpie, telling of his adventures, so plainly exaggerating that she soon grew weary of the bragging and arrogance, his insufferable maleness, and in the end she sent him away without the prize he had so confidently presumed would be his for a bracelet and a smile.

The town's incredulity, some of it good-natured and some of it not, only made Alberto believe her all the more. His grief subsided and his hopes were reborn. Harder than ever he worked with the nets and the lines; with greater and greater ardency he played his guitar each night at dusk, his passion so tangible that Lucia Luna would sometimes sing herself breathless and then stand on the rock and hug herself, eyes closed, so that Alberto knew his quivering notes had found their mark.

It was nearly a month later when the change began. As with most changes it came swiftly, not in dribs and drabs but in a lightning stroke, a stab in the heart. At midday a black storm ripped so quickly across the water that the men in their small boats had not a chance of outrunning it. It was as if the blue enameled egg of the sky had cracked open, and out sprang a thundering demon spitting waterspouts and sulfur.

The villagers' boats were tossed about like toys. The men shouted directions to one another but their voices were mere whimpers. Above them the sky blazed with lightning. On every side, waves rose up like walls, only to crash down atop them. For half an hour there was no color to the world but for the color of fire flaring in the snapping gray sheets of rain.

More than one boat capsized, throwing its occupants into the sea. For a while it seemed that men were being thrown into the ocean as quickly as their friends could scoop them out again, and no one knew, until one by one the boats grounded ashore and the men stumbled out to collapse breathless against the rocks, just who had been saved and who had been lost.

By this time, with the storm racing up the coast, leaving behind a shimmering lemon sunshine and the scent of sulfur, most of the village had gathered on the shore or was anxiously making its way down the slippery steep path. Upon spotting their husbands and sons each woman paused for just a moment, sucked in a lungful of relief, muttered a prayer of thanks, then hurried to embrace her family and to tease them about looking like mice the cat had held in its mouth for an hour only to spit out. Nobody noticed that Valencia Didión's pace grew slower and slower as she came down the path, or that she was eventually passed by everyone else making the descent. And nobody noticed that she finally came to a halt several yards from the bottom, that she stood there counting the boats and scrutinizing the shiny faces mingling ashore, or that she then lifted her gaze out over the water again, out to where the horizon became a dull line of blue atop the darker blue of empty sea.

Only when a tired fisherman with his grateful family turned toward home was she spotted, a figure frozen on the cliff path. Women spoke quickly to their husbands; the fishermen shouted to one another; eyes surveyed the ocean; heads shook. "No, I didn't see them, did you?" "Weren't they on your left coming in?" "When did you see them last?"

Within minutes the questions died. A handful of women embraced their men, then started up the path toward Valencia Didión.

She raised her hands as if to ward them off. "No," she said, slowly shaking her head back and forth, "no … no … not the niños too …" But the women converged on her all the same, they circled her, they bowed their heads against hers, they held her up in their embrace. She seemed to disappear for a moment, swallowed in the sympathy of others.

But then she pushed a woman aside and burst into view again, facing the shore. She seemed huge in her anguish, swollen by rage. "Where are they?" she screamed to the men below, not a question but an accusation. "Why didn't you help them? You helped yourselves, didn't you? *You're* all here! But where is *my* family?"

The men bowed their heads. They knew they had done all they could, yet her words stung like anemone spurs.

"Amiga," a woman said very softly, and put a hand to her arm.

Valencia Didión spun toward her, eyes flashing. "Where is *your* husband?" she demanded. She turned to the next woman. "And yours? Why is it that *your* children are all safe?"

Again somebody tried to comfort her with a touch, but she was beyond comfort now, still tumbling through the pit of her misery. She shoved the women aside and broke away from them, lurching back up the path, climbing as if through mud.

"We had better go with her," Rosario Morales muttered to the group.

"There is no telling what she might do," said María Quesada, a young woman who had been married less than a year. The others nodded, and a few moments later they began the ascent, some of them weeping as they walked, crying not so much for Valencia Didión as at the horror of imagining themselves in her place.

Moments later the rest of the villagers followed, the men dragging their gear, mothers clinging to their children. They came upon the group that had preceded them now stalled in the center of town, huddled along the edge of the street. Some stood poised as if to run, but nobody moved, nobody uttered a sound. On the peaked roof of the Luna house lay a jaguar, licking its paw.

Peña, one of the fishermen, whispered, "I have a pistol. Don't anybody move." He side stepped all the way to his own house three doors away, hurried inside, then returned a minute later with a rusty handgun. Hands trembling, he shoved a bullet into the chamber, then stiffly extended his arm, thumbed back the hammer, and fired over the crowd.

Several villagers flinched and tucked their necks, but the cat barely stirred. It licked its whiskers.

"Try aiming in the cat's direction next time," somebody whispered hoarsely.

"I hit him. I know I did."

"He didn't seem to mind it much."

"Shooting with your eyes open might help."

Inching his way closer to the crowd, Peña dug into his pocket for another bullet. He pushed it into place and cocked the hammer. The crowd parted, giving him a clear path to the front. He paused well to the rear and fired over their heads again.

This time the jaguar yawned, a gesture that caused a collective gasp to issue from the crowd. When the cat stood on the roof and stretched luxuriously, then swatted at a bumblebee flying too near, nearly everybody ducked. Peña reached into his pocket for a third bullet.

"Maybe you'd better stop before he gets angry," somebody suggested.

"I hit him right between the eyes! There's no way I could have missed."

"He must be swallowing the bullets."

Peña shuffled closer. He extended his arm and sighted along the top of the short barrel. "Steady," a villager whispered. "Steady … steady …"

This time after Peña shot, the cat looked down at him and growled.

"You are putting holes in the sky, cabrón."

But Valencia Didión, standing near the front of the group, spoke in a clear and unwavering voice. "You cannot hurt what doesn't die."

For a moment no one responded. Then a woman said, "Explain what you mean by that."

Valencia Didión turned to the crowd. Her eyes, as black and cold as agates, moved from one face to the other until they found Lucia Luna. "Ask the one from whose bedroom it came."

Lucia Luna was too stunned by this accusation to speak. But others in the crowd suddenly found their tongues.

"Look, she's right! Lucia's window is wide open!"

"And there's the cat directly above it."

"It's as if he's standing guard."

At that moment the jaguar leapt to the ground, landing softly beside the Luna house, on the same side as Lucia's open window. Instantly the crowd scattered, diving into doorways and behind corners. Alberto ran too, but after a few steps he glanced back over his shoulder and, seeing that Valencia Didión and Lucia Luna had held their ground, he stopped as well. Lucia was doing the practical thing of eyeing the jaguar, waiting for its next move. But the older woman, apparently indifferent to the possibility of a mangling, kept her eyes riveted to Lucia Luna.

It was an amazing stand-off that seemed to last forever, though Alberto was able to time the incident with his own heartbeats, which he could feel thrashing inside his chest. In spite of the fact that an eternity passed between each bruising thump, he counted only five. Then the cat tossed its huge head once and, its muscles rippling, ambled away—straight between the two women.

Alberto might have noticed Lucia Luna's eyes growing wide and the blood draining from her face had he not at that moment lost all capacity for observation. He stood paralyzed, unable to do so much as squeeze shut his own eyes as the jaguar loped toward him. When it brushed against his leg, arching its back like a house cat, it was all he could do to remain on his feet until the animal had turned away and trotted off into the jungle. Then Alberto's legs collapsed and he dropped to his knees.

Neither woman took note of him. Valencia Didión moved a step closer to Lucia Luna. "What is it you have against me, bruja?"

Lucia breathed twice, trying to calm herself. She glanced toward the jungle, saw only a riffling of damp leaves, and pushed a strand of hair out of her eyes. "I understand your grief, señora… But that doesn't give you the right to call me a witch."

Valencia lifted her head slightly and called out, "Did you hit him or not, Peña?"

From behind a doorway, he answered. "Two times at least! The first… I might have missed him by a hair."

Valencia's eyes returned to Lucia Luna, who bit her lip and shook her head in disbelief. "It was a wild animal, nothing more. I saw it for the first time just minutes ago, the same as the rest of you."

"The first time in the form of a jaguar, sí."

The villagers were coming back into the street now, venturing into the open. They regarded Lucia Luna with mouths ajar, eyebrows raised. She answered flatly, "Arcadio Martín was not a dolphin-man."

"We know that now," said Valencia Didión. "We know that he can appear in whatever form he chooses. And we also know that you are his concubine."

Lucia Luna, her face ashen, looked from one villager to another. "May I be damned in Hell if that is true!"

"You will no doubt get your wish," Valencia told her. She turned then to address the group assembling behind her. "I only wonder how many of us she will manage to take along."

With that, Valencia Didión stalked away. She was joined by several other women who, taking her by the arm or pressing close to her, accompanied the widow into the darkness of her home.

Lucia Luna stood alone in front of her house. Her mother and father looked out from a neighbor's doorway. "Surely none of you can believe such madness," she said.

There were a few mutterings, a few indistinguishable words of support. One person chuckled, then another. A handful of individuals started toward her. "What are we—a bunch of superstitious old women?" somebody asked. Lucia Luna smiled. A bumblebee buzzed once around her head. On its second pass, Lucia Luna swatted at it with an open hand, batting it to the ground. It thrashed in the dirt for a moment, reoriented itself, and took to the air again.

The villagers stopped in their tracks. For a moment there... wasn't there something familiar about the way Lucia Luna had moved, the sleek speed with which she had struck, the way her golden bracelet flashed like a yellow claw...?

One by one they backed away from her, grinning to show how little credence they allotted their fears, muttering apologies about how much work there was to do today, how busy they were. And when a jaguar growled from what seemed the very edge of the jungle, and a small black cloud of birds exploded squawking into the air, Lucia Luna soon found herself staring at an empty street. No one remained but Alberto, who, after a moment's reflection, wobbled to his feet and started toward her.

In his mind he was already sorting through endearments, searching for the phrase that would not only soothe her wounded feelings but bind her heart indelibly to his. He had nearly settled on *The world is filled with fools, bella, but the biggest fools of all are those who turn away from love;* had nearly advanced close enough to reach out and take her hand and awaken her from her trance of disbelief when, like bullies snatching a sweet from a child, her parents intercepted her. One on each side, they hurried Lucia away from him, they pushed her toward their home.

"It will pass, don't worry," her father said. "All things pass."

"You don't believe what she says about me, do you?"

"Of course not," he answered, his eyes on the ground.

"And you, mamá?"

"No, mi hija. A mother would never believe such things, true or otherwise."

Alberto watched as they disappeared inside the house. The door closed with no sound at all. Moments later Señor Luna appeared at a window; he closed the shutters and latched them. One by one the windows were sealed off.

Alberto stood in the middle of the street and felt the sunlight hot on his face. He smelled the mud at his feet. A bumblebee buzzed his head, darting at his eyes, but he did not have the strength to chase it away. All around him, from behind every door, voices muttered. He felt lightheaded, a peculiar and not unpleasant feeling of floating, but accompanied by a vague nausea. To spare himself the discomfort of falling he went down on his knees again, and then sat. To steady himself he held onto his ankles. *The world is filled with fools,* he said again and again, a partial prayer whose benediction he could not manage to recall.

<hr/>

It is said that good luck comes in trickles but that bad luck comes by the bucketful. In Mundosuave, the buckets were barrels. Whether the villagers were dipping into that black water of their own accord, attempting to quench some ancient thirst by immersing themselves in dream and exaggeration, or whether the incidents they recounted so floridly actually occurred, hardly matters. What matters is that the days passed and dragged the nights along behind them, and in both sunshine and shadow adumbrations and mists were seen, sinuous trails of foreboding, all thick with the dust of envy and fear.

Were the fishermen more nervous during the next few weeks, so that the swish of their nets and the slap of their paddles chased the fish out to sea? Did the sullenness of each bad day so add to the next that, before long, their small boats were preceded by a stench of failure as tangible to the fish as an oil slick?

The men, in any case, began to see faces in the water. Ribbons of seaweed were said to be strands of long black hair. Boats, it was reported, would rock back and forth for no reason at all. And when it came time each night to haul the meager catch ashore, few villagers lingered to enjoy Lucia Luna's singing or Alberto's accompaniment, both of which, no matter how brightly performed, sounded as lugubrious as distant thunder.

The situation on land was no better. The women went into the orange grove one day only to discover most of the fruit fallen to the ground, the skins split open, the oranges black with insects.

The women picked up one piece of fruit after another, examined each in disgust, threw it down. Valencia Didión walked along behind the others, looking like a banshee with her hair uncombed, her clothes wrinkled by a week of sleepless nights. But as the other women shook their heads in confusion, she nodded to herself and smiled.

"It was so cold last night," Rosario Morales said, and shivered at the thought of it. "I can't believe how cold it was."

María Quesada told her, "Three of my chickens were dead this morning. And there wasn't a mark on any of them."

The women kicked at the fruit, rolled them over with their feet. After a while María Quesada uncovered an orange that had been buried in the grass; only one end of the fruit was brown, the skin unbroken. She was about to slip it into her apron when she spotted Valencia Didión standing underneath a tree, staring into the branches as if praying for an angel.

"Amiga, look," María told her, and held out the orange, "this one isn't so bad. Here, you take it."

But Valencia, still smiling, did not lower her eyes from the branches. María looked up. Stretched out on the branch just a foot above her head, beginning to unwind itself toward her, was a long slender snake, dun with red markings.

"Ahh!" María cried, a short scream of surprise. She dropped the orange, seized Valencia's wrist and dragged her from beneath the tree.

A moment later María yanked out the crucifix that hung from a chain around her neck, squeezed it in her right hand and chanted "Our Father who art in heaven, hallowed be Thy name Thy kingdom come Thy will be done..."

All the while, Valencia Didión giggled softly.

———

The grandfather has been staring at the beach for such a long time that his eyes have begun to sting. He blinks twice and then rubs at the corners of his eyes, but he can coax no comforting moisture to soften his gaze. His tear ducts dried up a very long time ago. If he were home he would bathe his eyes in salt water, but he does not wish to go home just yet, there is still some light in the sky, still an hour or two of sunshine before the horizon will bleed like a wound that never heals, after which, in the indigo twilight, that clot of filthy rags will crawl off its boulder and drag herself up the steep cliff path to go home to sleep and, he supposes, to dream of music.

Sometimes it hurts too much to look at her. Sometimes he wonders if she is really there at all, if Mundosuave ever really existed. Maybe it is nothing more than a story he had been told, and the story has somehow gotten mixed into his life, like sugar stirred into water. Were it not for the boy, the old man might wonder if he too were not just a castaway from his own imagination. And now, in the boy's absence, it is too easy to let his mind drift off wherever it will, a chunk of flotsam for which the sharks of time have shown little appetite.

On a section of broken wall near his right hand, a small black caterpillar crawls. The old man bends over to have a closer look. He has become farsighted with age, and although he can clearly discern the outline of a ship miles away, he has great difficulty comprehending those objects right under his nose. Until he bends very close to the caterpillar, he thinks it is an inchworm. Now he sees the segmented body and the stiff little filaments of hair. It rears up onto its tail and sniffs him, their noses nearly touching.

"Where are you headed?" the old man asks. "It's a long hike to the end of this wall, believe me." The caterpillar bobs and nods, it scrutinizes him up and down.

The old man wonders what the caterpillar sees. Is the grandfather's face so close, so huge as to render it indistinguishable as such? Does his face look like a craggy landscape of some kind, his eye a dim sun? If so, the old man's breath must seem to the caterpillar a hot breeze, a scorching out of nowhere.

The grandfather turns his head slightly and peers into the sky. Do the things he perceives there really exist? A curved roof of blue … the creeping cataract of clouds. "Even those helicopters I hate so much," he muses out loud, and wonders what they might be instead. Motes of dust? Whirring bacterium?

When he looks to the stone wall again, the caterpillar is gone. Where could it have fled so quickly? And then he feels a tickle under the palm of his hand. He lifts his hand off the stone. A tiny yellow butterfly, no bigger than a moth really but as bright as a buttercup, flutters out. It soars straight toward his face, hovers before his eyes a moment, then makes a sharp banking turn and settles three inches below his right ear, its wings gently riffling the hair on his neck.

Suddenly a pinprick of pain shoots through the old man's neck, and, without thinking, he slaps at it. Since when do butterflies sting? he wonders. With three fingers he plucks it off his skin, brings his hand close to his face, and examines it. Why, it had not been a butterfly at all, but an ugly little tick. A shapeless little sac of tick that must have fallen from a tree and gorged itself on the grandfather's blood—blood which, now that the old man has squashed the insect, is smeared over his fingertips.

The grandfather shakes the exploded carcass off his fingers and onto the dusty tiles. Then he covers it with his foot. He does not want to have to look at it. He wipes his fingers clean on his trousers. A minute later, curious, he lifts his foot aside and is pleased to see that the powdery dirt has absorbed all traces of the violence; there is nothing beneath his shoe but a spidery crack in the clay tile, exactly what is to be expected of a tile that has seen so many years of dancing and stomping, of weddings and funerals and fistfights and parties. After all, the old man thinks, it's only clay, only a scoop of earth molded and baked and dyed to look pretty, and nobody in his right mind would expect it to last forever.

Day after day the fishermen of Mundosuave came home more frustrated and exhausted. They dragged their boats ashore, tossed their meager catch to the waiting women, then climbed uphill to grumble and sleep. Every evening Lucia Luna would be waiting on the rock, dressed in her cool white dress and anxious to hand Alberto his guitar. But each time, it seemed she was able to sing fewer and fewer notes before the beach emptied of her audience, before every villager had hurried away from her, up the path and past Valencia Didión, who had taken to peering down from the summit, arms crossed imperiously across her chest.

On that evening when, just as Alberto strummed his first chord for the night, the last villagers were already scurrying uphill, Lucia Luna did not even bother to open her mouth in song. For a moment her eyes flooded with tears, but she brushed the tears aside before they could stain her cheeks, and then her eyes shone with nothing but the gleam of anger.

Brusquely she stepped off the boulder and splashed ashore. Alberto watched her striding vehemently up the path, and he laid his hand across the vibrating strings. He slid off the rock and stood, the water lapping at his shins, but he could go no farther, could not take his eyes off Lucia Luna as, with head bent and body leaning forward, she charged toward Valencia Didión.

From the look of things, Lucia was not even going to stop before she plowed into the woman. But at the last second she did stop, with little room to spare. "You're responsible for this," Lucia snapped. "Your hysteria infects everybody."

"I have opened their eyes to you, bruja." Valencia's voice was flat. Her mouth held the disconcerting smile that often forms on the lips of the dead.

Lucia Luna appeared to see through that smile, to understand why it was there. Even from his position below, Alberto could see her expression soften, could hear the compassion in her voice. "Amiga, believe me, I share your grief. And if there were anything at all I could do..."

For a moment it seemed that Valencia Didión had been reached by these words. She blinked once, twice, and as if something rigid began to soften inside her, her head drooped just a bit...just enough that her gaze fell on the slender braid of gold hanging loosely from Lucia Luna's wrist. Involuntarily her hand fluttered toward the bracelet, wanting to touch it, to feel...and when her fingertip slipped under the delicate chain, still Lucia Luna did not pull away or resist, she allowed the jewelry to be admired. Two fingers then, beginning to lift, pulling so hard that had Lucia Luna not seized the woman's hand the bracelet would surely have broken. At this Valencia Didión's head snapped up again, eyes raging, and she spat in Lucia Luna's face. Alberto blinked as if he had been spat upon, and his heart jumped, and at the same time he dropped his guitar. It floated on its back in the shallow water.

Lucia Luna bowed her head and wiped the gob of spittle from her cheek. She then scraped her cheek a second time, this time using her knuckles. As if in slow motion she wiped her hand dry on her dress.

Then she lifted her eyes to Valencia Didión. "From this moment on," Lucia told her in a voice hoarse with restraint, "you grieve without my sympathy." She pushed the older woman aside and strode up the street.

"If you had any sympathy at all," Valencia called after her, "you would have killed me along with my husband and sons! So don't talk to me about sympathy, whore. You with your trinket bought with my children's souls. We have had all the sympathy we can stand from la puta del diablo!"

At this Lucia Luna spun on her heels, a movement so violent and abrupt that it startled Valencia Didión into a sudden step backward, which in turn caused her to stumble and fall. She came so close to tumbling over the edge of the cliff, crashing fifty feet down to the rocks below, that had she not fallen within reach of a firmly buried stone, she would have landed at Alberto's feet.

Now it was Lucia Luna's turn to smile. As she approached the widow, Valencia hugged the ground and cried, "Did you see what she is capable of? She's going to destroy us all!"

Lucia Luna squatted beside her. From behind their door-jambs and through the slats of their shutters, all Mundosuave held its breath and watched. A single nudge was all it would take to send the older woman to her death.

Instead, Lucia Luna held her right arm in front of Valencia Didión's face, her fist aimed at the sky. For a moment it seemed she was going to strike the cowering woman. But then, with a sudden quick tug of her left hand, she tore the bracelet from her wrist and threw it on the ground. "Now leave me alone!" she said.

A few seconds dragged past. Eventually Valencia Didión's hand crept out to cover the golden chain. Lucia Luna leaned close to her. "Never speak to me again," she said evenly. "Never utter my name, never look in my direction for as long as you live. Because if you do... if you do, amiga... it will be worse for you than you could ever imagine."

She held the woman's gaze until Valencia looked away, until she turned her eyes to the ground. Then Lucia Luna stood. Breathlessly she paused, gazing down at the sea. There stood Alberto, who, peering up through the tears in his eyes, beheld her as a shimmering angel. She pointed in his direction. "Your guitar!" she shouted.

He cocked his head, puzzled. Did she want him to start playing *now?*

"It's getting away from you!" she called.

Finally it dawned on him that the guitar was no longer in his hand. He turned to his left and then to the right, and there his instrument lay, riding the waves, slowly being drawn to sea. He ran splashing after it, dove in and swam a few strokes.

By the time he turned for shore again, only the still-huddled figure of Valencia Didión was visible above. Ten minutes later Alberto crested the path. No villager had yet come to Valencia's aid. He slipped a hand under her arm and escorted her home. Valencia Didión walked blindly, her black mantilla, her mourning shawl, wound tightly about her eyes, both fists clutched like ballast rocks to her chest, a glimmer of gold just visible between two fingers.

<hr>

When he tries, and sometimes when he tries not to, the grandfather can still see the way his guitar had floated on the low waves, the waves buckling under the curved wood, filing ashore one after endless other while the instrument, drawn apparently by some greater force, had bobbed and drifted in the opposite direction, a duck separated from its flock, a solitary seabird oblivious to the tide. How many times in the intervening years the grandfather has asked himself if it would have been wiser to have climbed aboard that seabird and allowed it to float him away to wherever it wished! How many times he has tried to imagine what those places might have looked like, what futures might have been his, what memories might now people his head in place of all these shadows and whispered regrets!

Wondering is the old man's vocation now; obloquy is his livelihood. He does not mind so much that he has forged his own fortune out of low-grade ore, but that, in doing so, his smoke and steam have contaminated the fortunes of others. That harridan on the shore below, for example—would she be better or worse off now had Alberto ridden his guitar into oblivion?

And the boy... It is too late for Lucia Luna perhaps, but what of the nieto? Is the old man poisoning him too? He can hear the boy returning with his friends now, the three of them laughing and talking excitedly as they approach the square. The old man turns to watch them. They are still in a hurry, as boys always are. Luis is carrying a badminton racquet and wearing a Chicago Cubs baseball cap. Ernesto walks with a bright orange inner tube draped over his shoulder. The nieto swings in his right hand a pair of tennis shoes with their laces tied together.

"Grab whatever you can carry," Luis says to the other boys as he strides past the old man and then hops the stone wall. "We'll meet back here in two minutes."

"And don't tell anybody else!" says Ernesto. He too vaults the wall, then trots nimbly toward his house.

The nieto pauses beside the old man. "You see what I got?" And he holds up the pair of Adidas sneakers.

The grandfather takes one shoe in each hand and considers them critically. The tread of each toe is worn smooth, as if the previous owner had walked only downhill, but there are no holes in the tread. "What did you trade?" he asks.

"Nothing important," the boy answers. A moment later he adds, "Just that piece of stone from the ruins."

"The one with the writing on it?"

"What good are scratches nobody can read?" He swaggers a bit as he speaks, but the swagger does not last as

long as the question, which trails off into a softness with
no authority.

The grandfather shrugs. There is no use chastising the
boy now. "There's still some good wear left in these," he
says.

"The thing is ... they're too big for me."

The old man looks at him as if to ask, Then why would
you trade for them? But he says nothing.

The boy says, "They might fit you, though."

The old man carries them toward his chair. "Let's see."
He picks his guitar off the chair and hands it to the boy,
then the old man sits down and pries the sandal off his
right foot. Unfortunately he cannot push his heel into the
sneaker. He removes the laces and tries again. This time he
is able to squeeze his foot inside, but it is an uncomfortable
fit. "My toes have their elbows jammed into each other's
eyes," he says.

From his pocket, the boy produces a penknife. He
opens the blade and hands the knife to the old man.

"You don't mind?"

"Your toes have to breathe, don't they?"

The old man pulls off the shoe. Holding it very close
to his face so that he can see it clearly, he slices an opening across the length of the toe, then folds back the flap of
leather as if it were an awning. He slips the shoe on again
and smiles.

As he is slitting the second shoe, Ernesto and Luis leap
over the wall and into the plaza, Ernesto carrying two dried
gourds and Luis a straw basket containing some dried ja-
lapeños, a clove of garlic, and a crayon sketch of Jesus his
little sister made.

Luis glances at the old guitar in the boy's hand. "Not
even gringos are that stupid," he says.

"I'm not trading this," says the boy. "I'm just holding it for a minute."

Ernesto asks, "So what are you trading?"

The old man slips the second shoe onto his foot. He stretches out his legs and wiggles his toes. The boy says, without looking at his friends, "I don't think I'll go this time."

"Why not?" Luis asks.

"I don't like the way they talk to us. Like we're little babies or something."

"What difference does that make as long as we get something good out of them?"

The boy shrugs. He rubs his thumb up and down a guitar string.

"Don't ask to use any of the stuff we bring back," Luis tells him.

The boy considers responding to this, but he says nothing. Finally Luis turns away. As he does so he says, "You're worse than he is, you know that?"

The boy watches his friends for a moment, then he sits cross-legged beside the old man. "My toes are smiling again," says the grandfather. "Muchas gracias."

The boy hands him the guitar. "Do you remember where we stopped?"

Now it is the old man's turn to look guilty. "Things have continued to happen in your absence," he says.

"I thought you were going to stop the story until I came back."

"If I could stop it, nieto, I would have done so a hundred years ago."

The boy sucks in a breath through his nose, then blows it out his mouth. "Where is it now?" he asks.

The old man leans forward slightly and lays a hand atop the strings of his guitar. He gazes across the top of the stone wall. He squints into the distance. "It is where the madness begins," he says.

In the center of the square several villagers stood in the twilight, necks craned, eyes watching the moon as if it were an egg about to crack, a strange reptilian egg the color of a dirty flame. A tiny, toothless vieja, the oldest woman in Mundosuave, sadly shook her head. "That moon is very sick," she said.

"It looks like one of our oranges," said her son, a boy of eighty-three.

The knot of villagers nodded and murmured. A shiver of expectancy ran through each of them. But what they were expecting, none could say.

Minutes later, out of nowhere, out of their very silence, it seemed, a shrill, high-pitched scream knifed through the gathering darkness. The villagers stiffened as if stabbed. The scream lasted only a second or two, a chilling eternity. And when it trailed away like a sharp blade drawn gently from their spines, nobody spoke for another half minute, nobody moved, nobody so much as shivered until the realization dawned that they were safe, unscathed, they had heard something unusual or maybe they hadn't. They searched each other's faces for vindication of their own ears.

The old woman's son said, "That was a nighthawk, I think."

Another man said, "It sounded like a rabbit to me. Caught between something's teeth."

"Rabbits squeal like babies," a woman countered, "not like … not like what I heard."

The vieja pulled her shawl tighter around her shoulders. She snuggled closer to her son. "For the first time in my life," she told him, "I am glad to be so old."

In the morning, a morning unusually clear and bright, as if scalded by the dawn, Alberto stood with the other fishermen and some of their wives on the edge of the cliff. Unlike the rest of them, who were all peering down, mesmerized, Alberto faced the opposite direction.

He stared at the blank face of the Luna door. He did not know whether he wanted that door to open immediately or to stay closed forever. Señor Luna was there in the crowd with him, his nets draped over his shoulder, and Alberto had already scrutinized the man's face, had with a glance seen his eyes go gray with dread. Alberto imagined that his own eyes must look the same, that the taste of metal in his mouth and the sour weight of his breath were shared by the father of the woman they both loved.

When the door to the Luna house came open, and out stepped a sleepy Lucia to gather wood for the morning fire, Alberto's first impulse was to shout at her to run. But behind her there was only jungle. In the foreground, a rock-strewn shore. And she was barefoot, she was helpless. With her hair yet uncombed and her face unwashed, she looked smaller than usual, younger, a little sister he might carry in his arms.

She took only half a step beyond the threshold of her door. Then, looking up, she saw the crowd, all but one back turned to her. Her father had left the house ten minutes ago; he should be in his boat by now, pushing off for deeper water. Puzzled, she considered the sky. It was clear, no sign of a storm. She walked toward Alberto.

"Qué tal?" she said.

At the sound of her voice, the crowd turned as one. At her approach the crowd split in half, appearing to open a path for her when in fact they only wanted to keep their distance. Alberto, ten yards from the edge, stood his ground, and it was him she came to first. "What's going on?" she asked again. He nodded over his shoulder.

Lucia continued past him. A moment before she reached the precipice, her father took her by the arm, turned her away. "Let's go back home," he said.

She studied him for just a moment, then pulled her arm free. Another step and she was standing on the edge. Below her lay the body of Valencia Didión, crumpled on the stones. She looked precisely as everyone had imagined she would when, just yesterday, she had nearly tumbled off the cliff, knocked down by an angry glance.

Lucia Luna sucked in a breath, her hand to her mouth. She felt suddenly nauseated and laid both hands across her belly. She moaned and pushed hard, trying to keep the sickness down.

Behind her, the crowd saw Lucia Luna's shoulders tremble, they saw her bend slightly at the waist, they heard a stifled sound. "She's trying not to laugh out loud," somebody murmured.

"She's nearly doubled up with laughter. Look how pleased she is."

Lucia Luna heard all this, and froze. Then, shoving hard on her stomach she pushed her shoulders back, she drew herself up to full height.

Even before she turned to face the crowd they had begun to move, backing away, stooping, reaching for stones. The fishermen drew their knives from leather sheaths and stood in front of their women. "You can't possibly think—" was all she managed to say before the words were strangled in her throat. Somebody touched her arm and she jerked violently away, she turned to strike him only to see that it was Alberto, his eyes soft with supplication and grief.

Almost instantly another pair of hands took hold of her other arm, and she spun toward him—her father. Then, as Alberto too took hold of her, she felt herself going limp with disbelief, and as she was hurried through the crowd that shrank away from them, hurried back toward Señora Luna waiting anxiously in the open doorway, Lucia Luna looked from side to side, seeing not an individual face she recognized as that of friend or neighbor, just a blur of fear and anger, to which she said, "You're crazy, every one of you. Every single one of you has gone completely mad."

Alberto escorted her as far as the threshold, where he was crowded away by Lucia's mother. The door slammed shut in his face then. The sound struck a blow to his heart.

Moments later he turned aside and headed toward his own house. He did not look again at the crowd watching him, did not wish to see their smirks of derision, their baleful eyes. The morning light glared off the trampled earth, stinging and hot though his own eyes were narrowed to slits. His pace quickened, he almost ran. He could feel a danger growing huge and agile behind him, like a giant serpent unwinding itself in the sun.

He heard his mother's and father's whispers as he lay awake through most of the night. He heard the whispers that rustled like cicadas through Valencia Didión's funeral the next day. The golden bracelet, that slender snake of richness, maybe with magical properties and maybe not, had not been found on her body.

Later he watched his neighbors sneaking in and out of the Didión home, heard the furniture being overturned, pots and vases turned upside down and shaken, broken, cursed at for their emptiness. If the bracelet was found, nobody admitted it. They knew on whose wrist it now flashed, they said. They wouldn't dare touch it themselves, they said, not even if it suddenly appeared at their fingertips. If anybody but the bruja herself touched it, they said, the bracelet would probably begin to writhe and hiss, maybe even rear back and strike. Had anybody thought to examine Valencia Didión's body for two tiny puncture wounds?

Gold or not, they said, they wanted nothing to do with that bracelet. They wouldn't mind knowing where it was, they said, just to stay informed. But did they desire it themselves? Don't be silly, they said.

And after the first hour or so of the ransacking of the Didión home, during which time people sneaked into and then out of the house trying to conceal whatever they had deemed worth stealing, after that, when they began to bump into one another rushing from room to room, when a kind of giddiness infected them so that chairs and dishes and finally even the mattresses were hoisted onto shoulders and carried in plain view from one house to another, the redistribution of possessions took on the air of festivity, a celebration of newfound wealth.

Finally Jorge Canales filled the Didión threshold with his voluminous bulk and announced himself the new landlord. He turned his old place, which was smaller and not so well-maintained, over to his nephew, who was twenty years old and grateful to have a place of his own. And by the second day after Valencia Didión's plunge onto the rocks, the town of Mundosuave seemed—except for the sound of Jorge Canales methodically digging up his floor, and the complaints made in various households regarding the inequitable disposition of the Didión estate—as tranquil as ever.

A woman who had lingered too long at a neighbor's house hurried home in the dark. As she crossed the plaza she happened to glance heavenward. The moon looked bloated and misshapen, about to burst. At that moment a mosquito pricked the side of her neck. She turned her head in reaction to the bite and slapped at the insect, and in that instant she thought she saw Arcadio Martín crouching on the low stone wall, just a glimpse before he leapt from her grinning like the devil, his hand to his porkpie hat.

She gasped, she blinked... had she seen what she thought she saw? A chill ran through her; the mosquito bite throbbed hotly. She sensed a presence in the black corners of the plaza, something hiding in the trees. Panting for air, hearing the rasps of her breath as if they were footsteps dragging behind her, she peered out the corners of her eyes at the Luna home—just in time to see something flying from Lucia's window, an enormous black shape, greasy wings flapping! The woman wobbled to her knees, she fainted on the stones. A dragon-shaped cloud scraped across the face of the moon...

A young man slept beneath an orange tree in the stultifying heat of a Sunday afternoon, a film of pulque at the corner of his mouth, an empty gourd in his hand. The grass tickled his cheek, grass like long slender fingers, a lover's playful touch. The man smiled and moaned. Lascivious fingertips glided over his cheek and jaw, they traced a curving line down his chest, drew a circle on his belly, wiggled between his legs. He groaned sweetly and pushed his hips against the hand. Sleepily he tried to open his eyes to see his lover but his lids were heavy, they would barely yield. Through a blur of lashes he beheld her, the wondrous breasts as huge as a young man's dreams, the low-cut white dress from which they wanted to spill. The breasts glowed through his lashes, they pulled at him, twin moons, his body a tide of desire, heavy but buoyant as he struggled to raise his mouth to her, toward one of the nipples pink and bright peeking out at him.

To lift himself up he raised his heavy arms to where her neck would be if only he could see her. He looped his hands around what he thought would be her raven hair. But instead his hands touched something hard, a smooth cold shell. His eyes opened wider now, they unstuck, and he looked up just in time to see a scorpion's tail as big as a tree limb hovering above Lucia Luna's head, her stinger flicking from side to side, her red mouth grinning, eyes glowing orange.

The tail lashed down over her shoulder, the stinger jabbed at his head, nicking his ear. Again and again he tossed his head from side to side, again and again the tail stabbed down, missing him by the width of a hair. He tried to throw her off, to buck from beneath her, but her hands were strong, she pinned his shoulders to the ground, she rode him, she ground her hips into his groin. And even as he felt himself huge inside her the tail stabbed again and again at his head, his violent writhing arousing her even more, so that she bucked harder, she groaned, her claws dug into his shoulders...

He awoke screaming, clothes drenched with perspiration, trousers wet. Already there were people running toward him, coming to see what all the noise was about, eager to believe the confused recounting of his attack.

〜〜〜

Señora Luna faced the serape that hung as a door over the threshold of her daughter's bedroom. In her hand was a plate of food—three warm tortillas, beans and two fried eggs and salted tomatoes. Señor Luna sat at the tiny kitchen table, watching the blanket for a sign of movement, his own plate of food untouched.

For weeks now they had been denied even a glimpse of their beautiful daughter, not so much as a sleepy smile in the morning nor a truculent nod at night. Shortly after the funeral for Valencia Didión, Lucia had made herself invisible. She had stopped sitting around the corner of the open front door, listening to the gossip. She had stopped strolling out into the night for a breath of fresh air, only to run home with a stone bruise on her shoulder or head. She believed that if she disappeared from view completely, maybe the village would stop talking about her.

Instead, the rumors grew. Every household had its theory about what Lucia Luna was up to in her privacy. She was studying witchcraft, gathering her dark powers. No, said others; she was no longer in the Luna house at all but had left only her voice behind to fool everybody while she ran off to consort with the spirits. No, she was weaving porkpie hats. She was praying. She had lost all her hair and was ashamed to show herself. She was encased in a cocoon from which she would soon emerge sporting oily black wings, talons and fangs.

Her parents, who could not resist peeking in at her from time to time, claimed that all this talk was nonsense. She was sick of being harassed, they said. She would sit on her bed for hours at a time, combing her hair and singing softly to herself.

But even this was little more than rumor. Recently Lucia Luna had asked for tacks, but refused to say why she needed them. So her father had gone about the village begging for a handful, explaining that he needed to shore up a sagging roof board. He returned with an assortment of tacks, nails, and rusty pins. With these Lucia Luna secured the serape to the inside of her doorjamb, so that not even her mother and father could peek in at her.

"Here is your supper, bella," the señora now said as she slipped the plate of food beneath the blanket's bottom flap. She waited, poised on one knee, her hand still on the lip of the plate. Half a minute later there came a shuffling of feet. Still she did not withdraw her hand. And a moment later she was rewarded with the touch she needed to reassure herself, Lucia's hand closing warmly over her mother's for just a second, then pulling the plate away.

"Gracias," Lucia said.

Señora Luna returned to her place at the table, pulled her plate up close, looked down at it, and sighed. The señor and señora looked at their beans and at each other. They missed having Lucia seated across from them, the focus of their attention.

It was not long before there was another scraping sound behind Lucia's door. Her mother looked just in time to see the empty plate come sliding out. Her father, who moved a bit slower, asked in a whisper, "Did you see anything?"

Señora Luna rose heavily from her chair. She blinked away the same tears that came to her eyes several times each day. "I saw what I always see. My daughter's hand. The tips of her fingers."

From behind the serape Lucia said, "More tortillas, por favor. And more eggs and beans, if there are any."

"That hand has a big appetite," said her father. Then he rose too, picking up his own plate. He slid it beneath the blanket. "Here's what's left," he told her.

"Gracias, papá."

"De nada, chica."

Mother and father returned to their seats at the table. She slid her plate of food toward him. He took a bite of beans, chewed slowly, and handed the fork to her.

"Yesterday," Señora Luna told him, and whispered so that her daughter could not hear, "Rosario Morales came up with a new theory."

"Rosario was always an imaginative one."

"She said that our daughter has turned into an enormous black widow spider."

"Even as a little girl, Rosario was afraid of spiders."

"She said that one of these mornings Mundosuave will awaken to find that Lucia has spun a gigantic web over the entire town."

Señor Luna did not have enough energy left to lift a last forkful of beans to his mouth. Tragically he said, "If you ask me, our daughter has spun her web already. Unfortunately, I think it will trap no one but the spider herself."

Outside the front door, which although latched tight allowed cracks of light and noise to come and go, Alberto gritted his teeth and shook his head in refutation. No, he would never allow misfortune to visit his beloved. With guitar in hand he crept around to the shadows at the side of the house and leaned close to Lucia's shutter. He listened to the sound of her chewing, a mastication as delicate as that of a silk worm. He closed his eyes and imagined her lips moving against his, her tongue slurping feverishly in his mouth.

After a while she softly belched. Alberto wiped the spittle from his lips. Smiling dreamily, he held his guitar across his chest. His fingers were as light as butterflies on the strings, and the voice that answered from the opposite side of the shutters was as soft as the powder of a butterfly's wings. For an hour he played and Lucia sang in secret concert, their music so hushed that to any ears but their own it was indistinguishable from the distant lapping of the surf and the first dim twinkling of the evening's stars.

"In this manner," the grandfather says, "the months dragged by. Not once did Lucia Luna step outside or throw open her shutters. In the meantime, every misfortune large and small was attributed to her. In her absence, even the heat and drought became her doing."

"It was during this time," the boy quickly adds, because the grandfather's voice has slipped into a melancholy register, a familiar but dangerous place which, the boy knows, the grandfather likes to slide into, and, once fully ensconced there, is difficult to extract, "it was during this time that you learned to go without eating."

"There was not much to eat anyway. So I gave it up entirely."

The boy, by gazing unblinkingly into the old man's eyes, can see Alberto still posted at Lucia's shuttered window, stalwart and devoted, a sentinel of loyalty. "By denying your body," the boy says, "you hoped to whittle your spirit to its finest point."

"To make of my soul an arrow, sí. An arrow so slender and sure that, when released, it would sail unerringly into the very navel of her heart."

The boy nods solemnly. He does not always understand the old man's metaphors but even in the absence of understanding there is empathy. He likes the music of the grandfather's voice and sometimes the music has a meaning of its own.

"In those days," the old man continues, "even after what had already begun, I think we all thought of time as an endless parade of forevers. The possibility of drastic change was just another story, like the cities that were supposed to exist on the far side of the ocean."

"Things are different now," says the boy. "Awake or sleeping, I dream of little else but change."

The old man lays a gnarled hand on his shoulder. "As well you should, nieto." Miles away, deep in the jungle, a bulldozer sounds its warning bleat. "I only wish you did not have to keep watch over your dreams alone."

～～～

The light of dawn, the grandfather says, had not yet found the Quesada house when Arsenio, María's husband of less than a year, came creeping toward his bed. María lay on her back, hands clasped over her chest as if neatly folded in place by an undertaker, her breathing as sweet to Arsenio's ear as a cat's purr. He loved her for being asleep just now, just as he had prayed she would be, and he was so moved by the weighty thrum of love in his chest that he almost leaned over and kissed her for being such a thoughtful wife.

He decided, however, to postpone the kiss for a minute or two. There would be plenty of time for kissing after he was safely in bed. He began to undress, easing off one shoe and then the other, wincing at the sibilance of his socks as he peeled them over his ankles. Then he shed his trousers, carefully placing them in a twisted mess beside the chair where he tossed them every night. Next he removed his shirt. He flinched each time he popped a button through its hole.

Relieved to be naked, he smiled. One small tiptoe closer to the bed and he could ease himself in. For half a minute he stood near the edge of the bed and pondered whether to place first a knee or a buttock on the mattress. He finally opted for a knee, and, drawing in a deep breath, slowly raised his right foot off the floor. Just as he attained the stance of a flamingo, María's eyes flew open and she sat bolt upright.

"Did you have a nice night, rooster?" she seethed, her arms still folded atop her chest.

Arsenio froze in place, except for the darting of his eyes and the frantic twitching of a hamstring muscle.

María leaned toward him and pointed a finger in his face. "And don't tell me you've been outside counting the stars, because I counted them all twice already!"

Arsenio stood motionless a few moments longer. Then his eyes rolled back in his head and his eyelids fluttered. A second later he pitched over backward, crashing to the floor in what appeared to be a dead faint.

María took her time climbing out of bed. Then she stood over her husband, looking down. Even in the dimness of pre-morning she could see a vein throbbing in his forehead, his hands clenched at his sides. María crossed to her kitchen, then returned with a pitcher of water. Holding the pitcher as high as she could reach, she dumped the water on his face.

Arsenio sat up sputtering, waving his arms, trying to look in all directions at once. "What? What?" he cried. "What in the name of—" Just then he happened to spot his wife. He bobbed his head back and forth, squinting so as to focus in on her.

"Heart of my heart," he asked in a soft, confused voice, "what are you doing out of bed? What am *I* doing out of bed? Where did all this water come from? Is the roof leaking again?"

María shook the ceramic pitcher in his face. "No, but your skull is going to be leaking soon."

"Where are my clothes?" Arsenio asked. "And why are … oh, I feel terrible, my head is killing me." He clutched his head and swayed from side to side. "Somebody, please, tell me what's going on here."

María swung the pitcher at his head. He ducked away in the nick of time.

"You are three seconds from going to sleep forever, that's what is going on!" she told him. "Who were you with, cabrón? Name the whore! Who besides me is stupid enough to lie down with a jackass?" She swung again, this time nipping a small chunk from his ear.

"Wait, wait!" Arsenio cried. "I think I'm remembering something now!"

"Remember, too, that I am not the idiot you are hoping I will be."

"I remember it clearly now, I do! I know exactly what happened tonight—it has all come back to me in a flash."

María stood with arm cocked and pitcher at the ready. Arsenio scuttled backward, out of her reach. Then he pushed himself to his feet. Gingerly he crossed toward the bed. "I remember … we had supper, as wonderful as always. What you can do with a small piece of turtle meat never ceases to amaze me."

As she walked toward him, he spoke more quickly. "After supper we made love. And that too was wonderful. The best. Soon afterward, you fell asleep."

"It was in the middle of it that I fell asleep," María said. "Actually, at the beginning."

"In any case … that was when she appeared. Right here, at the foot of the bed!"

"And who is *she*, rooster? Your fairy godmother?"

Arsenio looked from one corner of the room to the other. He leaned toward his wife. "The bruja," he whispered. "Lucia Luna."

At the mention of Lucia's name, María Quesada's eyes grew from slits of suspicion to round stones of terror. Arsenio nodded, his own eyes wide. "Sí, in our very own house. Like a ghost she appeared." Warily he turned toward the door, as if afraid of what he might see.

"At first there was only a strange green mist," he explained. "It seeped in through that crack there. And came floating over here to the foot of the bed. And began to take shape as a woman."

He rubbed his eyes. His gaze grew distant and vacant. "I kept telling myself it was only a dream. But not even in my dreams could I imagine a body like that..."

"Like what?" María asked.

"Madre de dios, such miracles of flesh!"

"She was *naked?*"

"Such wonderments as I have never seen—" He heard the pitcher whistle a low note and he dove for the bed, the blur of María's arm riffling his hair. On the bed he rolled over quickly. "Nor ever want to see again, esposa! I tell you it was a horrible, horrible beauty! I tried with all my strength to look away!"

"How many times have I warned you to quit staring at women? Haven't I said it would get you in trouble some day?"

Arsenio nodded. "But those breasts," he told her, "they *glowed,* mi amor. Like devil moons they glowed! I only wish I could describe for you the hypnotic effect of such a terrible sight."

"You've described enough already. Tell me what happened next."

"Next?" he said. "The rest is...clouded, like muddy water. All I remember is that she took me by the hand and said, 'And now it is *my* turn, caballo.'"

"She called you a stallion? It must have been very dark in here."

"As a matter of fact, the glow from her breasts illuminated me from head to toe."

"Are you sure it wasn't *cabello* she said?"

"Why would she call me a hair? That doesn't make sense."

But María, thinking out loud, said, "If she had appeared in the home of Fuentes, perhaps, then sí, caballo…"

"What was that?"

"Hmm?" said María. Then, "Continue with your story! And quit stretching the truth."

"I wanted no part of her, I tell you that in all honesty. But she was strong, stronger than ten men. She dragged me kicking and screaming down to the beach."

"How loud did you scream?"

"Loud enough, I thought, to wake the dead. But it soon became obvious that she had placed a curse upon my voice. I could hear it, but no one else could."

"And when she had you on the beach?" María asked.

"It was awful. Too terrible to speak of."

"Speak," she said.

"She forced me to satisfy her. All night long, in every position imaginable. I was powerless to resist."

"And did you satisfy her?"

"I am ashamed to admit that I did."

"She must know something I don't," María said. "Tell me the rest."

"There is nothing more to tell. She took everything I had, and then some." Despite himself, a smile formed on his lips. "Even now, I can still see those devil moons of hers…swollen with desire…pulsing with the hot blood of—"

This time he did not hear the pitcher coming. He heard the explosion against the side of his head, and the tinkling rain of pieces as they scattered across the floor. The blow knocked him sideways off the bed, where he landed on his hands and knees. He tried to hold the floor in place as it swung wildly beneath him.

"She has no right to stoop so low," María said. "Caballo, my foot!" Saying this, she stomped across the room and snatched a machete hanging by a leather thong off its nail in the wall.

Arsenio looked up just in time to see her fling open the door and storm out into the heavy pink mist. He struggled to his feet, fumbled for his trousers and, pulling them on, lurched after her.

"Come to think of it," he called, "I never did get a very good look at her face! There was the fog ... and those blinding devil moons ..."

Just as he reached the door, María came striding vehemently back inside. She pushed him out of the way, then hurried about the room, pulling open drawers until she found her crucifix on a necklace and put it on. Next she picked up her Bible. Tucking it under one arm, she lifted a wreath of garlic off the wall and draped it over her neck. Then she gripped the machete and, holding it outstretched like a sword, again marched through the open door.

Arsenio staggered along behind her, feeling his head for blood. "To be perfectly honest, I doubt that I ever once even looked at her face ..."

The mist was cool and palpable on his skin. It refreshed him sufficiently that he could distinguish the shadow of his wife hurrying ahead. "I mean who knows?" he called after her, trying to whisper and at the same time to turn his wife around. "Maybe it was just a dream. And how could you blame me for what I dream? It's not as if I dream about her on purpose—"

Suddenly she was standing there in front of him, unmoving. She had come to a halt just ten yards from the

Luna home. "Ah, good," he said breathlessly, "you've come to your senses. So let's just let bygones be bygones and—"

"Shhh!" she told him. She raised a quivering hand and pointed the machete into the mist. Arsenio followed with his eyes the curve of the blade—just in time to see the sleek shadow of a jaguar slipping into the jungle.

"You saw where it came from?" María asked.

"I barely saw where it went."

María tiptoed close to the side of the Luna house, Arsenio at her heels. "You see?" he whispered. "Lucia's window is closed up tight."

"So was our door." She put her eyes to the shutter and tried to peek between the slats.

"Come away from there. You're going to get us both in trouble!"

María turned to him and smiled. Her eyes were hard and slitted again. A moment later she crept toward the front door.

"I am ordering you to get back here!" Arsenio said.

María slipped her machete between the door and the jamb. As she sawed at the slender latchboard she said, "You think I am afraid of her?"

"I think maybe you're too stupid to be afraid."

Just then the machete cut through the wood. María withdrew the long knife and spit on its blade. "She will not throw *my* body over the cliff." She eased open the door and crept inside.

"If she does," Arsenio whispered hoarsely, his throat constricting, "don't expect me to be standing down there to catch you." And he waited on the threshold, his body turned sideways, balanced on his toes, poised to run.

"There's something I've always wondered about," the boy says.

"Wondering is good for the spirit. As long as you don't overdo it."

"There are parts of the story where you don't appear. I mean after all, you couldn't have been everywhere at once. And yet you seem to know every little thing that happened."

"People did a lot of talking in those days."

"They even told you their thoughts?"

"You shouldn't be so concerned about technicalities," the old man says. "You get stuck on minor details."

"I don't do it to annoy you, Grandfather."

"You're too sophisticated for your own good, that's all. It's not your fault, but there's nothing we can do about it now."

"I never used to wonder about such things. Only in the past year or so have they begun to bother me."

The old man nods. The boy is no longer a child. Mundo-muerto is no longer a child. Sometimes the old man wonders if he is the only child left in the entire world. There is no one to play with anymore. And I, he has to admit, even I am losing my enthusiasm for play.

"If your enjoyment depends upon an explanation," the old man tells the boy, "then I will provide you with one. Where I did not see or hear the things that happened in Mundosuave, or was not told about them by somebody else, some of the things came to me in dreams, and others came to me the very first time I told the story. Even now, new things are coming to me with each retelling. It's one of the reasons I keep telling it."

He puts a hand on the boy's arm and gives it an affectionate squeeze. "Though I have always appreciated having such an attentive audience."

The boy, however, appears troubled. "Does this mean that you've been making the story up as you go along?"

"Not only me," the old man says, "but you. Every time you look for Alberto or Lucia Luna or Arcadio Martín in the shimmer of my eyes, you see a bit more of the story. Your looking makes it appear. So, in this regard, you are just as important to the story as I am."

"So the story isn't true after all?"

"Of course it's true. Even the parts that we haven't yet discovered or spoken of are true. There are a hundred people in Mundosuave who I never bring into this story, but this is their story just as much as it is mine and yours. Every story with more than one character in it is more than one story. And every one of them is true."

"I'm not sure I understand," says the boy.

"Nobody ever asked you to understand, niño. Understanding is for the scientist. For the banker, and the road builder. For us, in the end, understanding isn't what's important."

"Then what is?"

"To keep telling the story," the old man says. "To allow the story its opportunity to speak."

From inside the front room María Quesada could see two doorways hung with serapes. She went to the one on her left, from which the blanket hung loosely, and lifted a corner of it aside. Atop the narrow bed in that small room the señor and señora lay curled together like cats in a rain storm, both of them snoring loudly.

"Pssst!" hissed Arsenio from the dooryard.

María waved her hand at him, motioning for him to go away.

"You're going to get us killed!"

But María had fixed her gaze on the second blanket now. It was stretched as tight as a drumskin on three sides of the doorjamb. Only by lying on her belly and putting her nose to the floor could she see inside the room. But nothing she saw in this manner satisfied her.

María stood then and pressed the tip of her machete to the taut cloth. "No no no *no!*" Arsenio whispered. He clutched his head in both hands as if it were about to leap off his neck in fright.

María paid no attention. She made a small incision in the cloth at eye level. She stuck a finger in this incision, pulled it into a hole, and put her right eye to it.

By now Arsenio had dropped to his knees in the door-yard. With hands clasped in front of his face he alternately prayed and peeked around the corner to see what insanity his wife would perpetrate next.

When María turned away from the peephole to convey the fruit of her observation to her husband, her eyes were as wide as sand dollars. Unfortunately, Arsenio was immersed in fervent prayer. María smiled at her timorous husband; she turned and smiled at the punctured blanket. Finally she placed the tip of the machete in the hole she had made, and, her smile widening with the effort, drew the knife down with a sharp, firm movement, splitting the blanket in half.

At the sound of rending cloth, Lucia Luna stirred. She had been lying on her side on the thin mattress, naked, facing the door, her left arm draped over her eyes. As the serape split with the sound of a dry cornhusk being shucked, she flung back her arm. Her eyes blinked heavily. She drew her knees to her belly and covered her belly with her hands, but there was no concealing the swell of her abdomen or the damp brown shine of her distended skin.

María turned her head slightly so as to call out over her shoulder, but she kept her eyes on Lucia Luna. "Come look at your devil moons now, esposo!"

She strode through the split serape and, smirking grimly, crossed the room to throw open Lucia's shutters. Lucia was still trying to come awake, to separate this unreasonable invasion from the surreality of dream.

"Everybody!" María called through the window. "Everybody, come look! Come see why the whore has been hiding from us!"

"Mamá!" Lucia called in a voice so tiny it surprised even her. "Papá?"

"Her belly's as big as a pumpkin!" María shrieked. "La puta del diablo está encinta!"

As the cobwebs of sleep were brushed away, Lucia's confusion turned to anger. Awkwardly she rolled out of bed, making no attempt to cover herself.

"Get out!" she cried. "Hyena, get out of my room!"

She lurched toward María, who in response hurled the Bible at Lucia's face. But the deftness with which Lucia batted aside the Holy Book without missing a step brought another surge of fear. María dropped the machete clattering to the floor, then dove headfirst out the window.

A moment later she was standing in the middle of the street, screaming at the top of her lungs. "Wake up, everybody, wake up! Come look at the bruja now! She screws a dolphin and sleeps with a jaguar and last night she raped my devoted husband Arsenio! Who knows what kind of seed is growing inside her?"

As for Lucia Luna, her anger sustained her for only the briefest of moments. She collapsed in sobs beneath her open window, curled like a newborn against the rough and splintered wood. She looked up for just a moment when she felt the blanket from her bed being draped around her; looked up to see her father's funereal face.

Señora Luna was screaming something indecipherable, shoving at Arsenio Quesada and two or three other villagers who were crowding through the door to get a peek at her daughter.

Lucia yanked the blanket over her head. Her feet stuck out at the bottom, and no matter how she tried she could not tuck them out of sight. She could hear her father just above her and could feel his legs bumping against her as he pushed villagers away from the window. But every time he shoved one person aside, two more filled the window frame. In a matter of seconds all of Mundosuave was trying to pour into the house from one opening or another.

Alberto had been awakened abruptly from a troubling dream in which Mundosuave was an island bobbing on a sea of boiling red lava. In this dream it was Alberto's job to pole the island to safety, but every time he shoved his pole into the lava, the wood burned and disintegrated up to his knuckles. All the while the town was shrieking and fiery drops of lava were sputtering against him, scorching his skin.

In his dream he heard Lucia's name called out, and in the irrationality of the dream it seemed that she was crying to him for assistance. He was well into the street, running barefoot and bare-chested toward the crowd, before the lava stopped raining down on him and became the thinning pink mist of dawn. But even as he pushed his way up to Lucia's window, he had made no sense of the scene. He acted out of instinct and emotion only, as desperately as he had in his dream.

One glance at Señor Luna's face told Alberto all he needed to know. Like a wild man he began grabbing at his neighbors and yanking them away from the window. He shoved and kicked and spun until he could get both hands on the shutters and bring them together. As he pushed them toward Señor Luna's waiting hands, a look passed between the boy and the man, a look deeper than words, sadder than tears and more knowing than gratitude. And then the shutters slammed tight.

For a moment no one spoke. Alberto turned away and walked back toward his home, back toward his parents, who were running toward him. He was oblivious to the excoriation being heaped on him by his neighbors. Oblivious to his parents' puzzled looks. Oblivious to the dawn and the fecund scent of the sea and to everything but the heavy gray ache that had become his drowning heart.

⸻

As always at this point in the story, the old man pauses. It is not a voluntary rest he takes, but one dictated by the story itself, which, wanting like all of us to find a state of comfort, a degree of happiness, stops at this crossroads to look in every direction, to consider its path. It knows that there is only one path it can take, the familiar one, trod again and again, and it knows that the other roads, once bypassed, have ceased to exist except in wistfulness, the mirage of cómo que.

Yet the urge to rewrite itself is strong. The story wishes it had moved more carefully in the beginning, had been as vigilant then as it has grown to be too late. If given the chance to start anew it would be conscious of the consequences of every casual step along the way, every incidental pebble kicked.

Unfortunately there can be only one beginning. To be followed by this incessant retracing of footsteps, this scrutiny of a passage already made but not yet finished. And this is the story's only hope, its only energy... that it is not yet finished. That a meticulous consideration of its trail of misery might insure that the end of one road can become the beginning of another.

In the meantime the old man waits, both hands quiet and flat on the face of the guitar. The boy, like the leaves of the jungle behind him, feels the shadows deepen, and trembles slightly, resigned to another night. Despite his age he is still too young to know that the clot of heaviness in his chest is a sadness he feels not for the old man but for himself. He does not know that he leans forward to cover a gnarled hand with his own not just for the grandfather's comfort but for his own as well. "Have you forgotten what happens next?" the boy asks.

"To forget would be a blessing I do not deserve."

"Are you tired?"

"As tired as the hills, yes. As tired as the sea."

"If you wish we could stop for today."

"For today, and for twenty thousand yesterdays," the old man says. Briefly he presses his other hand atop the boy's. "Unfortunately," the old man says, "to stop is not a choice we have the right to make."

The day of Lucia Luna's unveiling, no fishing was done, no work in the gardens, no picking of fruit nor hunting for wild pigs along the edges of the jungle. Talk and speculation were the only labors of the day; what to do with this evil in their midst? Some of the fishermen thought she should be taken far out to sea and hacked into pieces and dumped overboard. Return both Lucia Luna and the perversity she carried to the depths of the ocean, they said, from whence it had come. Unfortunately, to do so meant that they would have to lay hands on her, and everybody knew how strong she was, stronger still, no doubt, with so much evil on her side. So this, now that they considered it, seemed an unworkable plan.

Others thought she should be burned alive. Her smoke would purify Mundosuave and call the fish back to its waters. But what if, somebody suggested, what if her smoke hovers over the town in an oily black cloud, a cloud so thick that no wind can blow it away, so dense that no sunshine or rain can penetrate it?

Somebody suggested they send an emissary to inquire of what it would take to placate her. What were a couple of chickens a month, or a goat, or a net full of fish, if it kept her happy? And to this came the answer, Have you forgotten the Didións, hombre? One whole family gone, wiped out. Does that sound to you like the work of a devil who will be satisfied with a goat?

Alberto offered to marry Lucia Luna, and with the sanctity of holy vows to cleanse her of all wrongdoing, and to be a father to her child. But even before he finished with this declaration he was laughed into silence, and he stumbled away blinking back the tears, his ears burning to the cries of Cretino! and Estúpido!

It was a day when tongues fluttered faster than reason, and because of this the day passed quickly. The night was a calm one, filled as it was with the reassuring image of Lucia Luna reduced to a cowering heap of turgid breasts and desperate sobs. Even the agents of evil, it seemed, could be shamed.

Then came morning. Just as the heat was beginning to rise, the door to the Luna house was flung open. Out stepped Lucia Luna into a bright, clear day. Like the Lucia of old, of that long ago time only a few months earlier, she stood with her sturdy legs slightly spread, hands on her hips, face raised to the sun.

Her dress was as white as confidence. Her raven hair had been combed until it shone. Her black eyes flashed with the purity and hardness of onyx. Her parents, unable to convince Lucia of the prudence of continued seclusion, slouched in their chairs, made feeble by love.

To the townspeople who first spotted Lucia Luna as they straggled toward the cliff path or tossed potato peelings to the chickens or merely stood in their hardscrabble yards to scratch themselves and wonder how to spend another day, this unexpected appearance of the bruja both shocked and excited them, as the appearance of any demon would.

Except for the bulge of her stomach, they might have been able to shake their heads in wonder of their past fears and midnight thoughts. They might have forgotten themselves and called out to her, "Buenos días, paloma!" and with their smiles asked her to forgive their embarrassing superstitions. She was as beautiful as ever, as erect and proud. But there was, they noticed upon second glance, a challenge in the way she held her chin so high; a ferocity to those flashing eyes. And that belly...

That same white dress, just months earlier, had hung on her like the dress of a goddess, so perfectly turned to every curve and convexity of her body. How snugly it had lain over the slight mound of her abdomen back then, on that hillock every man's eyes had scaled only to slide into the sweetness of the valley suggested below. But now that tempting mound seemed grotesquely swollen, the white cloth straining over it, as taut as tripe. They could almost feel the dark and terrible thing it hid.

Lucia was beautiful and horrible in her shamelessness. Every person who looked at her felt a stab of terrible passion, a desire as sudden and scalding as blood.

Lucia Luna took another step beyond her doorway. She raised her arms to the sky, she stretched from her fingertips to toes, reaching so high that some who watched imagined she was about to pull the sun down atop them.

María Quesada, who with a bucket of water and a rag had been wiping the night's dust from a clay icon of the Madonna stationed in her yard, turned to her husband sitting in the doorway. "Do you believe this?" she asked.

Arsenio said nothing. The moment he saw Lucia and felt himself leaning toward her, drawn as if by the tide of her breasts, he jammed his hands behind his hips and scooted backward inch by inch, scuttling toward darkness like a clumsy spider.

In the meantime, Lucia Luna turned on her heels. She spun once, a slow pirouette, causing her dress to billow around her thighs. Women gasped, and men laid scarred hands upon their hearts. Down the center of the street she began to stroll then, her eyes focused straight ahead, a wry smile on her lips.

"Puta," a man hissed.

She turned her head slightly—it was Jorge Canales, that stubby gourd of a man, watching her through his open window.

"Is the dolphin-man built like a real man where it counts, bruja?" he asked. "Or does he blow air through that hole too?"

Lucia Luna tossed back her head and continued on. "What you have between your legs," she answered over her shoulder, "is less than a peanut compared to his."

At the next house, crouched in the yard, a middle-aged woman looked up from the fruitless tomato plants whose wilted leaves she had been nipping. "What kind of stinking fish are you growing in there?" she asked.

Lucia continued to smile, leisurely strolling, both hands on her belly. "Whatever it is, it's sure to be better-looking than those frogs that call *you* mother."

Next she came abreast of María Quesada's yard. Here Lucia paused. She turned to face the woman who, with a dirty rag dripping in her hand, crouched tight against the Madonna. Lucia fixed her with a smile so cold that Arsenio Quesada gave himself a final shove backward and rolled away behind the door.

Lucia said, "We used to be friends, María. But this morning you showed what kind of friend you are. You violated my privacy, you called me a witch and a whore, and now I am here to respond in kind." Lucia extended her arm and pointed a finger at the trembling woman. "From this moment on, may your womb remain as empty as your heart. My hope for you is that you grow old and barren and alone, betrayed by everyone you know just as you have betrayed me."

With that, Lucia Luna turned away. María Quesada clung to the clay statue; she could not stop shivering.

With each step through Mundosuave Lucia felt lighter and stronger. If the town insisted on her being a witch, a witch she would be. To her delight she found that a mere glance could send some of her neighbors scurrying for cover. Others crossed themselves or knelt as she drew near. Once she had passed them by, however, they seemed emboldened by the fact that they had not been struck down, and they joined the group that followed her at a distance like a nervous pack of children taunting a rabid dog to bite.

Now and then, from the safety of the crowd, a voice called out to her. She answered without turning or breaking stride, her smile intact. "Tell us what other animals you have soiled yourself with, ramera."

"Ask your husband. He was there."

"There is only one thing to do with a woman like you."

"Only one? But your sons and husbands have found a hundred things to do."

A small mongrel came running up to her out of a yard. Lucia paused. She knelt down to pet the dog. When it lay in the dirt at her feet and rolled onto its back, Lucia Luna scratched its hairless belly.

"Have you slept with that one too?" somebody asked.

She laughed softly. She was thinking that she might leap to her feet and spin around and send them all scattering, but then the thought came to her that maybe she had gone far enough, it was time to get back to normal again, to make peace with her friends. She patted the dog's belly a final time, then began to rise.

At that moment a stone flew from the crowd and struck her bare shoulder. She gasped in pain and clapped her hand to the wound and felt the blood beneath her fingers. It was then María Quesada spoke.

"Remove the curse from me, witch! Or else I will cut out your heart and stomp on it."

She strode to the front of the crowd that had gathered behind Lucia Luna. In one trembling hand María Quesada clutched a machete. In the other, tucked under her arm, was her whitewashed statue of the Blessed Virgin.

Lucia Luna felt blood oozing down her shoulder. It found the slope of her spine and trickled into the small of her back.

"It's too late," Lucia answered. Even as she spoke she regretted her words, but she could not stop them. Her nostrils flared with anger. "Your insides are filled with chicken excrement," she said. "It grows harder by the minute."

Horrified, María dropped the machete and clutched her abdomen. She staggered forward a step, doubled over the statue. Then she dropped to her knees, moaning, and clawed at her belly.

Lucia laughed.

Another stone flew from the crowd. It struck Lucia on the arm and spun her to the side. Before she could rise she was struck again. And soon there was a fourth stone flung. A fifth. A sixth.

"It was a joke!" she cried. On her hands and knees she looked toward María Quesada, who now lay on the ground, curled around the clay statue. All around her stood the villagers, grim-faced and silent. Many of them were armed with rocks or sticks. Some of the fishermen held gaffing hooks; others had unsheathed their knives.

"She was teasing," Lucia implored, "and so was I. María and I are like sisters, we would never hurt one another. I sang at your wedding—remember, amiga?"

María spoke to the ground. "One by one, she will murder us all."

"She's imagining this! *I have no power!*"

The crowd stood as one, unmoving. And the longer they stood there staring at Lucia Luna as if she were something abhorrent, something unnatural, like an insect they wanted to squash, the hotter her temper flared. As always with Lucia Luna, anger soon supplanted fear.

Struggling to her feet, her legs wobbly, she raised a shaky finger at the mob. "I will not let you do this to me. You people are insane. There is not one among you who truly knows what I have done or who I—"

A hand closed over her mouth and silenced her. She spun to face the attacker, only to see her father's eyes, tear-

ful and beseeching. "Shhh," he whispered, "shhh. For the
love of God, chica... silencio, por favor." Gently he lowered her to her knees, and he knelt beside her.

In her father's arms she began to tremble. Her own eyes
mirrored his, luminous with tears. Señor Luna gathered his
daughter in his arms, held her against him, shielded her
with his love. Looking over her shoulder, he spoke softly to
his neighbors.

"My friends, mira, take a good look at her. My daughter is not a witch, can't you see that? She is just a girl who
has gotten herself in trouble."

He stroked her raven hair. He kissed her head. "Let me
take her home again, please. I promise you she will never
leave the house. You will never hear another word from her,
I swear."

Still, the crowd said nothing. There were some who
wanted to turn away then, who knew they should creep
back to their homes and shut the door and consider in darkness what things they had almost done. There were some
who shivered with embarrassment; others who wanted to
laugh out loud but were afraid of being the solitary voice.
They had come to a place, the grandfather says, where if
they wished they might have turned back into the sunlight,
and in the warmth of good humor and forgiveness a balance might have been restored. They stood there on the
verge of conciliation, and had there been one brave soul to
step forward and take the first blame, to say *I, for one, will
not agree to this any longer,* the others might have followed.

"But even I," the old man confesses, "even I remained
in the safety of the crowd. Not because I was a part of it,
but because I lacked the confidence in my ability to turn
them around. Unfortunately, in the end it does not matter
why we choose not to act as we know we should. It is still
cowardice, no matter how we color it."

In the stillness of the morning, with nothing discernible but the buzz of insects and the occasional shriek of a gull, the crowd held its breath and waited. The small dog that Lucia had petted just minutes earlier now came trotting up to her as she huddled against her father. The dog licked her foot, then nuzzled her hand.

"Florito!" its owner called. "Come here!"

The dog turned toward the voice. Flicking its tail, it moved a step away from Lucia Luna. It searched the crowd for the face of its owner, its tail snapping the hem of Lucia Luna's dress.

Tentatively she put her hand out to pet the dog. But before her fingers could find the animal, a stone flew from an unseen hand and cut across the knuckle of her middle finger, sending a stab of pain up Lucia Luna's arm. "Basta!" she cried.

Almost simultaneously her father shouted "Los asnos! Let me see who threw that and by God I will—" But before he could finish his threat, two men rushed forward and seized him by the arms. In an instant they dragged him away from his daughter, and soon other men emerged from the crowd to engulf and overwhelm him.

"She's just a girl!" he cried as he was shoved to the ground. A dozen feet pinned him in place. "Have you all lost your minds?"

Jorge Canales, wielding a long pole with a gaffing hook attached to one end, stepped toward Lucia Luna. "It is out of your hands, my friend," he said to her father. "Be quiet now. And pray for her soul."

Lucia Luna crouched alone in the dust, poised on her fingers and toes as if she might at any moment pounce on Jorge Canales, though all she really wanted was escape. He inched closer, jabbing his gaffing hook at her face.

"Protect your throat, Jorge," someone told him. "She'll go for your throat."

Lucia scuffled backward. He jabbed again, and this time she tried to snatch the pole from Jorge's hands, but only managed to gouge a deep cut across her arm. When he lowered the pole and took aim on her abdomen, Lucia Luna covered her belly with both arms and rolled into a tight ball.

"Perfidia!" screamed a neighbor, and hurled a stone against her rounded back.

"Unholiness!" cried another.

Lucia Luna squeezed shut her eyes and felt her mind go black with disbelief. She didn't know whether to lie still like an armadillo or to jump up and run. She could hear the shrill voices of her mother and father crying out for sanity, for mercy, and she could distinguish other familiar voices too, voices shrieking curses, sanguinary and cold. It all seemed very distant and yet overwhelmingly near; she felt the stones pelting her, she smelled the dry dust churned up by her crablike movements, she felt the weight of her belly dragging her toward the ground. It all conjoined in the heavy clot of nausea that sat in her chest and in the sour taste of bile that burned her throat.

Even the warmth and the weight of the pair of legs now straddling her seemed somehow distant. She had not seen Alberto shove his way to the front of the crowd, had not seen him rush forward and wrestle the gaffing hook from Jorge's hands. And now, as Alberto stood over her, a slender, bare-chested boy gripping a long spurred pole, every muscle tensed, she did not know if she was being protected or attacked. A growing part of her no longer cared, but only wished for an end.

"I will cut in half anyone who touches her!" Alberto shouted.

"Come away from her, niño."

"She is a walking debasement!"

"She left us no choice. Look what she has done to our town!"

Lucia turned her head and peered up at him; a bloody hand clutched at his leg. "No one will harm you," he told her. "I swear it."

"Alberto, listen to me," a woman from the crowd implored. "She has put a spell on you too, can't you see? Because she is afraid to die alone, she wants to take you with her."

Alberto looked down at Lucia Luna; the confusion in her eyes nearly made him swoon. "If that is what she wants," he said, "I go gladly."

A moment later he faced the crowd. "But so will some of you. I will make certain of that."

Again there was silence. It lasted so long that a soft chirping of birds filtered into it, and Alberto smiled for a moment, so sweet was their song. Then the crowd parted slightly to make way for a young man named Poco, an infant-faced nineteen-year-old nearly twice as big as Alberto.

He walked slowly, a shy and lumbering gait, and grinned to himself as he approached the tip of Alberto's gaff. In Poco's hand, drawn but pointed at the ground, was the gleaming saber he wore on his hip in the fashion of the conquistadors he had once heard stories of.

"Buenos días, Alberto," Poco said. He came so close that Alberto was able to rest the heavy hook against Poco's chest. Alberto said nothing, and the older boy smiled, his face as round as a moon.

"I've brought my saber," Poco said.

"So I see."

"You know how I use this on el tiburón?"

"I have seen more than one shark die at your hands, sí."

"There's a place just above their eyes," Poco told him. "You have to be very precise or you will never reach the brain. The blade will break on the skull."

"I've always been amazed at your skill," Alberto said.

"If I had been born farther inland, I might be a famous matador by now."

"I don't doubt it for a moment."

"That's very nice of you to say." Poco looked at the ground and sighed.

A few moments later, he looked up at the sky. "I have been told that, to make a perfect kill, the blade must go in just behind the bull's neck, so that it severs the spinal cord. Death is instantaneous."

Alberto nodded.

"A man, I've been told, can be killed in the same way." He looked Alberto in the eye. "So that there is no pain, amigo."

"I hope it is true."

"And then the blade will continue on. Because the true target is not you, you understand, but the witch. Unless, of course, you will agree to step out of the way for a moment."

"Even if my feet agreed to move, my heart will not. It is as heavy as an anchor right now. I couldn't budge even if I wanted to."

"I suspected as much," said Poco. "And so, just think of the sharks I have killed, and rest assured that I will be equally kind to you. All in one swift movement it will happen. In the blink of an eye."

"If that is what you choose to do, Poco, there is nothing I can do to stop you. All I ask is that you do not call her a witch again. I consider it a personal insult."

"It is not my intention to insult you, Alberto. I apologize."

"Gracias."

"Por nada," the big man said. He and Alberto smiled at one another.

Then Alberto leaned forward and laid his gaff in the dirt. He spread himself atop Lucia Luna, but without putting his weight on her, his neck across hers, their heads side by side.

She lay very still, her ear pressed to the earth, and listened to the slap of the waves against the shore. Her breathing had fallen into the same rhythm as the waves, and when she closed her eyes she imagined herself to be drifting out to sea, sinking slowly under, Alberto's body a warm cushion of deepening water.

"Cretino," somebody muttered, but Alberto continued to smile. Lucia's hair smelled like the night itself.

And as Poco walked slowly around the huddled bodies, looking for the perfect point of entry, Alberto waited for that moment when a few drops of his blood would be thrust by saber into his beloved's heart—a moment, Alberto knew, that would join them forever.

"And all this time, Grandfather—weren't you frightened?"

"I think I was too busy being a fool," the old man answers.

"It seems to me that you were more of a hero than a fool."

The old man shrugs. "It's hard to say. The definitions keep changing. Today's hero is tomorrow's idiot, and vice versa."

"Surely you don't regret saving her life."

The old man gazes across the low stone wall. He does not have to be able to see around corners or down steep inclines to view in his mind's eye a weather-beaten crone in a time-tattered dress, the sinew that had once bound her bones to one another now rotted away, dissolved, her skeleton held in place by the gristle of bitterness, confined in a loose bag of skin through whose veins only venom now flows, her seat a water-smoothed boulder that has weathered the elements far more gracefully than its occupant has.

"Regret," the old man says, "is God's business, not mine."

The boy scrapes the toe of his shoe through the plaza dust. He considers the slender trail he has made. And then he obliterates it. "Sometimes I think there must be no God."

The old man shrugs. "It seems a logical assumption."

"Wait!" came a voice from the back of the crowd, so sudden and resonant that the crowd gasped in a single response.

Even Poco was startled. With the tip of his saber poised half an inch above Alberto's neck, so close that Alberto could feel the cool vibrations of death emanating from the steel, Poco held his breath, eyebrows cocked, and waited.

"Please wait! Slow down!" Alberto's father cried, hands raised above his head, patting the air. "This isn't necessary! There's another way!"

In the midst of the crowd he disappeared for a moment as he knelt beside Señor Luna, who was still being held to the ground. He whispered something in the man's ear. Señor Luna thought for a moment, then nodded.

Alberto's father stood and whispered into the ear of the man next to him. That man too nodded, and turned to his neighbor. Within seconds the entire crowd was whispering excitedly.

Alberto's father pushed forward and approached Poco. He motioned for the tall boy to bend down, and thus Poco was made privy to the secret.

He nodded enthusiastically, a broad grin on his face. A moment later he slipped his saber into the leather sheath that hung from his belt. Playfully he tousled Alberto's hair.

Alberto stiffened at the touch, still waiting for the deadly thrust. Poco's hand withdrew, and still Alberto remained motionless. He waited so long that he began to wonder if maybe he was dead already, killed instantaneously and without pain, just as Poco had promised, and if waiting like this for something to happen was what death is all about. He wanted to lift his head and see what the countryside of death looked like, but he was afraid that if he wasn't already dead he would disturb Poco's aim and end up merely paralyzed. So he continued to wait. He waited until his body grew so stiff with the tension of waiting that his limbs trembled and a prickliness crawled up his arms.

All this time Lucia Luna lay motionless beneath him, completely still but for the subtle rise and fall of her breathing. He was as close at that moment as he had ever been to her, their postures very nearly intimate, and he was reluctant to abandon this position for any reason whatsoever.

He drew away from her eventually only to keep from falling atop her, his limbs now numb from immobility. He lifted his head and saw the street surprisingly empty. Only two couples remained. Alberto's father was standing there with his arm around his wife, who stood leaning against Lucia's mother, who was being held up by Lucia's father. Tears streaked all their faces, yet all four parents smiled.

Alberto's father walked over to the boy and helped him to stand. "Ya basta, chico. Everyone is gone."

Alberto was dazed. Was this the afterlife? If so, it wasn't nearly as crowded as he had expected. "What's going on?" he asked.

Señor Luna told him, "They were just having some fun with you. It's over now." He then bent over and gathered his daughter into his arms. The señora helped by picking up Lucia's legs.

"That was a pretty good joke," Alberto said.

Cradled in her father's arms, Lucia Luna squinted up at him, blinking.

Her mother kissed Lucia's cheek. "It's all over, mi hija. We can go home now."

Alberto, braced by his father on one side and his mother on the other, watched Lucia Luna being carried away. At one point she turned in her father's arms and, with eyes half-closed, smiled weakly at Alberto. He nodded, too tired to bow. For just an instant he was flooded with joy and energy, and was about to slap his father on the back and say *What a good joke that was!*, but then he noticed Lucia's lovely white dress shadowed with dirt and blood, and he saw the black stains of dust-thickened blood on her hand and shoulder, and with the sun burning in his eyes as bright as a saber, his legs suddenly collapsed, and he fell down hard on his knees.

The boy gazes into the old man's eyes and sees another boy standing there in the indigo light, in a twilight as still as his sadness. In that boy's left hand is the old man's guitar, but shinier, new; in his right hand, an orange. This second boy, Alberto, faced the closed shutters of Lucia Luna's window, his chin lifted slightly, eyes closed, head cocked to the side. The jungle just twenty yards away smelled damp and fecund, as dark as loam.

From the other direction came a sea-scent as fresh as his love, yet as old as the mud of desire. In Alberto's nostrils the scents combined to become the scent of Lucia Luna, her natural perfume. Every breath he took was another breath of her; awake or dreaming he breathed her in, his ether and his air, his sustenance and his poison.

"What is he doing now?" the old man asks. He tries to hold his head steady and to keep his gaze fixed on a single point on the horizon, but there are three turkey vultures gliding in lazy spirals out beyond the cliff, three graceful frowns of black whose vigilance is difficult to ignore.

The boy leans close to see the Alberto of the old man's eyes. "He is standing at her window, watching time go by."

The grandfather nods. "Days and weeks limped past as I stood at that window. Like mourners to the grave they marched, month after month. And every footstep left its mark on me."

Haltingly, Alberto came forward then. He leaned his guitar against the house, and with his fingertips tapped lightly on the shutter.

As the grandfather waits for Lucia Luna's response, he says, "During the nights, I did not even try to sleep."

"Why sleep," says the boy, echoing the words he has heard a thousand times before, "when there is no sunrise to awaken to?"

Again Alberto tapped the shutter. He put his mouth to the slats and whispered. "I've brought you a piece of fruit, bella. It is small, I'm afraid … but without blemish. It took me all afternoon to find such a fruit."

The boy feels a shiver of anticipation race through him. "Now the shutter will open," he says.

And as half the louvered door creaked outward, and Lucia's hand appeared between the two halves, palm up, the boy for a few dizzying moments does not know if it is he who places the orange in her hand and then leans forward to brush his lips across the very tips of her fingers, or Alberto. He is sure, a moment afterward, when he runs his tongue across his lips, that the taste of her fingertips lingers there, as salty as a sea breeze.

"Gracias, Alberto," Lucia said. Her hand withdrew, and the shutter creaked shut again.

"It is nothing," the boy and the old man say.

Alberto reclaimed his guitar then and very softly he began to play. Each chord was as light as the smallest puff of smoke, so that no sooner was it born than it rose between them, trembled sweetly for an instant, and dissolved, not a trace of it discernible to any ears but their own.

Lucia's voice too was soft as she sang, but it harbored too much misery and joy to go unnoticed by the other villagers. Although night after night the sound never registered to the villagers as the voice of Lucia Luna, everybody in town felt its presence in the air.

A fisherman might look up from repairing his net and, regarding the sky, suggest, "I think we should work closer to shore tomorrow," only to be told by his partner, "I was thinking just the opposite. I have a feeling we'll be lucky further out."

A woman might sneak up behind her husband and slip her hands inside his shirt and whisper something to make his eyes come open wide, while another wife might sneak off somewhere alone to remember a boy she used to love.

Children were known to whimper in their sleep, or to laugh out loud for no reason.

When Lucia Luna sang, there was more than the scent of sweet smoke in the dusky air, though no one could have named it or even guessed that it was there.

"For nearly five months," the grandfather says, "this was our routine. To everyone else in town Lucia Luna had become invisible, a memory, the unnamed chill that made them shudder at night. As if by agreement nobody mentioned her name. So it was easy for me to stand unnoticed by her window in the magic light of sunset, for no eye ever gazed in that direction, but deliberately sought the distraction of one's foot or callused hand or the watery blister of a rising moon."

"And all that time," the boy continues, "you took no nourishment but for the dulcet whisper of her song."

"I never even thought of eating, it's true. Mere food and drink would have been putrid in my mouth, so filling was the manna of her voice and her scent."

"And as you played for her, something would happen to the light…"

"Can you see it?"

The boy searches the old man's eyes. "Sí, abuelo."

Layer by layer the twilight was transformed, darkening, thickening, as if midnight had come four hours early. Then each note from Alberto's guitar became another star that flickered brilliantly for a moment and then melted, flattened out, and oozed across the sky in a stream of translucent blue, quivering gold, vermilion, orchid, apricot, or sapphire. The moon itself became a pearl of dew that spread like syrup across the firmament, a milky radiance atremble with song.

And soon Alberto felt himself to be floating. Like a shimmering bubble the earth drifted away beneath his feet and he was left there to stand on its afterglow. In his rapture he saw Lucia Luna's shutters waft open, and on her song she floated out to him, singing for his ears alone. She was dressed in a gown woven from the moonlight, with fuzzy filaments of stellar dust trailing behind. Her breasts were round, her belly flat, and as Alberto played she floated around him as weightless as an angel, her gossamer hands stroking his face, his chest and shoulders, his stomach and thighs.

"As I played," the grandfather remembers, "through her voice and the answer of my guitar we made such love as I could never describe. I cannot tell you the sweet madness I felt as I filled her with my song, or as the muscle of her heat pulled me into her, throbbing its sorrow. My hands, as they rode the strings of my instrument, as they slipped and stroked those humming sinews, discovered every curve of her body. Every warm slick mystery was unveiled to me each night... until I was gasping from every pore, breathless and spent. So as not to fly off into space in a million pieces I had to step away from her finally, gasping for air, and allow the last sad chord to fade away."

Reluctantly then, Alberto opened his eyes. He saw the world unchanged, enveloped in the orchid light of reality, beautiful but flat, illuminated only by a sickly moon in one corner of the sky, the sun's last stain of blood in the other. As for Lucia Luna's window, it was shuttered tight. The air was hot and as dry as dust. Alberto could hear her sobs from the other side of the shutters, the helpless moans she tried without success to stifle.

He lay a hand on the slatted wood. "Your tears are as sharp as knives, Lucia. Tell me what to do."

She answered with more weeping.

"Did you have another nightmare?" he asked.

From the edge of her bed, where she sat facing the window, Lucia Luna choked back a sob. "Last night I dreamed of the jaguar again," she told him. "I dreamed that I awoke to find him standing between my legs. With a sweep of his claw he tore me open. Then, as I lay there screaming, he shoved his muzzle inside me and he devoured my baby."

Alberto squeezed shut his eyes, grimacing; her fear was his torment, her misery his pain.

"And this afternoon, when I was napping, I saw myself out walking on the street. Suddenly, without warning, a horrible spasm took hold of me, and I gave birth. There on the ground lay a half-formed cherub. It lay there fluttering like a butterfly, its tiny heart on the outside of its chest, its wings beating at the dust which then settled back on top of it, burying it alive…"

Alberto shook his head, his throat too thick with tears to speak. He looked up at the moon—a watery egg excoriated with cracks. With both hands he wiped the tears from his cheeks. "You must try not to dwell on such things," he said. "Dreams are nothing, they're only… only dreams. Think, as I do, of how it will be when all this has passed."

"They are plotting something terrible," she whispered hoarsely. "I know they are!"

Alberto shivered. "Open your window, bella, and I will carry you away from this place. I will never let anyone harm you again."

Suddenly her voice was angry and shrill. "Where would you take me?" she demanded. "Do you have a house of your own somewhere I don't know about? Do you have a boat of your own? A trunk full of money?"

Stung by the truth of her words, Alberto felt small, a boy, an ineffectual dreamer. "Tell me what to do, Lucia. Whatever is best for you, tell me and I will do it."

There was a pause then, a silence that trembled. When she spoke, her voice was soft. "Go find the peddler Arcadio Martín. And bring him to me."

Alberto was dumbstruck. He felt as if the back of his skull had been whacked with a board. There was a ringing in his ears.

Stunned as he was, the click of her shutter latch did not seem real to him. Nor did the quality of the air, hanging before his eyes like a film of pale blue water through which he watched the shutters slowly open, revealing the face he had been dreaming of for months, the face he saw no matter where he looked, awake or dreaming. Yet it was a different face too, the same but unfamiliar. There were those same hypnotic black eyes he knew better than his own, as limpid as tide pools . . . but red-rimmed and puffy. Her face was bloated and shinier than he remembered, her complexion pallid, her hair dull and brittle, an abandoned nest.

Lucia Luna stared at him as if she had forgotten how to blink. "He lives, he said, in Nuevas Alijas."

Alberto felt the world tilt on its side. He leaned to his left, so as not to slide off. "I have . . . never been to Nuevas Alijas," he stammered. "It's a . . . a long way off. At least fifty miles through the jungle. Longer if I . . . follow the coastline."

Her voice was as certain as his was halting. "I see. Your promises do not reach that far."

An urge to cry welled up in him, an impulse to run away to some cool dark corner and hide in sleep until this burden passed.

"What do you think?" Lucia asked. "That I am going to marry that pig? For all I know, he has five or six wives already."

"Then why . . . ?"

"Bring him back here for the people to see! Let them get a look at him. Let them tear him apart for all I care. Maybe then they will leave *me* alone."

Alberto turned his head by a few degrees and regarded the jungle. In the dying light it looked impenetrable, a wall of tangled vines and ferns and grasping branches that would swallow him up and entomb him, his body a day's meal for some beast. He knew there were narrow paths through the jungle, and in fact he had ventured into it on numerous occasions, had felt at home there in the broken shafts of daylight and steamy ground, playing, hunting wild peccaries, fishing in its streams. But Lucia Luna was asking him to delve ten times deeper than he had ever gone before—and for what? She looked twice her age now; she looked more frightening than appealing.

Desperate for an excuse, he turned sideways and considered the ocean. Three turkey vultures circled above the shoreline, a shoreline Alberto knew to be treacherous and clogged with boulders, making walking impossible. And he knew in an instant that he could never row to Nuevas Alijas alone, fighting winds and tides and currents all the way. Besides, to steal a boat, in those lean times especially, would be criminal.

"If only I were a few years older," he muttered.

With difficulty Lucia Luna leaned over her windowsill. She extended her arm and, reaching as far as she could, touched her fingertips to his hip. He gasped and stepped away even before he turned to look at her.

But now she was smiling, and the smile transformed her somehow, it softened her features. The longer he looked at her the more clearly he saw Lucia Luna as he remembered her in his dreams. There was still something wild about her, yes, but she had always been unpredictable, and that in large measure was her beauty, that you knew she could kill you with her smile, she could tear you to pieces with her all-consuming eyes.

"Come stand closer," she whispered, and he moved within her reach again. She slipped three fingers over the top of his trousers and exerted a gentle pull. "Closer. Please don't make me have to reach for you, Alberto. I'm so desperate to have you next to me."

He advanced to within a foot of the window. Lucia Luna eased back inside, only her arm protruding. She rubbed a hand across his stomach and waist. "Mmm," she said, and allowed her hand to glide down his thigh, to slip to the inside, to climb upward again.

"Oh," she said, and Alberto echoed her.

"I don't know why you think you need to be older," she told him, panting, breathing rapidly through her mouth. "To me you feel like a man already. A man fully grown."

"Sí?" he asked, too breathless for thought.

Her hand pulled at him. Her head lifted back and her eyelids fluttered as if she might faint. "Just to think of the things you could do to me," she said. "It makes me weak just to imagine it."

She moved her hand in a small firm circle, fingers cupping and squeezing. Alberto closed his eyes and, with knees trembling, rocked his hips toward her.

But then her hand slipped away, its warmth disappeared.

He opened his eyes to find her fully inside the window again, both hands pressed to her chest. She had never looked so beautiful to him, never so wild and helpless.

"Please say you will be my hero," she whispered, eyes shimmering. "Please, Alberto. Will you do this thing for me?"

Only then did he realize that he was still holding his guitar. He let it fall to the ground. "Inmediatamente," he said, and stepped toward the window, and threw one leg onto the sill.

Lucia Luna thrust a hand against his chest. "I mean," she said, "will you go to Nuevas Alijas for me?"

"Sí," he said. "Whatever you ask." Again he began to pull himself through the window.

This time she placed both hands on his shoulders and pushed him down. "When you return, my brave one."

He had neither the words nor the breath to refute her. His hands rose heavily, reaching out, wanting another touch. But all they encountered were rough slats of wood as the shutters closed once again, his fingers pushing into the narrow openings, grasping at air.

From behind the shutters, her lips brushed against his fingertips as she spoke. "The moment you return with him, Alberto, I will be yours. To do with as you desire. Para siempre, mi picador. For ever and ever."

He gazed again at the jungle. Perhaps, in the daylight… "What if Arcadio Martín does not wish to return with me?" he asked.

"I don't require his compliance, only his body. You may bring it here in whatever condition you choose."

The grandfather pauses for a moment to allow a shiver to pass. Then he says, "I had never been a lover of violence, and the thought that Martín might resist me was enough to give me a chill. But then I told myself, You are a good talker, you will find some way to convince him. And I turned in a daze and headed back toward my parents' house, thinking I should get a few hours of sleep before my journey began."

"You did not even realize that you had left your guitar behind until you heard Lucia Luna whispering your name."

Alberto returned to the side of the house and picked up his guitar. "Yes?" he asked.

"Never forget," she told him. "Todo por amor."

"Sí," Alberto mumbled. "Everything for love."

With that he turned and walked away. "But instead of going straight home," the grandfather says, "I was drawn to the edge of the cliff. There is something comforting about the ocean, you know. Especially when the sun has entered it, and the surface of the water still glows with their pleasure. And I sensed that I might not see this moment again in a very long time."

Alberto stood on the edge of the cliff, gazing into the distance. By staring into the pool of soft light at horizon's end he encouraged himself that he would be strong in the morning, that although weakened now, barely stronger than an infant, he would rise bold and new to confront the challenge of another day. He would find Arcadio Martín and one way or another convince the peddler to return to Mundosuave. The months of horror would thus be erased; the time lost, regained.

Alberto smiled to himself, feeling stronger already. Only when he came back from the sunset to stand on the cliff again, only then did he look down. There on the shore were the three turkey vultures, no longer graceful, ugly waddling shadows tearing chunks of meat from an overturned turtle that had washed ashore. The ungainly birds grunted and hissed at one another, their hooked beaks dragging the turtle carcass a few inches this way, a few inches that.

Within moments another vulture flapped down and like a bleary-eyed drunk sidled up beside these three. Alberto looked away; more birds were coming in from the east. He turned and ran for home, hoping to get inside before the sky turned black with pinions.

A restless night, a night of shadows and whispers, of fears and doubts.

When he slept, Alberto dreamed he was awake, lying trapped between a clay sky and a bed of ochre mud. Flat on his back he could raise his head only an inch or so before it bumped the sky. With his knees he made shallow indentations in the clay, then gripped these bowls with his fingertips and slid himself through the muck. If he lay still for long the mud began to harden around him, and then he had to pull with all his strength to break himself free. And so he kept punching indentations into the sky and pulling himself beneath them, slide after monotonous slide, all in the vague hope that he might discover a break in this gray cloud and be able to stand again, look around, perhaps see beyond the tip of his nose.

Weak from his dream-labors, Alberto arose at dawn and sneaked from his parents' home. He looked in on them before he left, he watched them sleeping, but in the end he had no thoughts that would fit into a whispered goodbye and he left them with his silence.

The machete he tied to his belt with a leather thong slapped against his leg as he walked. It pulled on him in a way his guitar never had, making him feel off balance. Even the mist seemed different to him this morning, it smelled both sweeter and sadder, redolent with the scent of the ocean, which is that of a mother's grief. He wondered how tomorrow morning would smell when he awoke in the depth of the jungle. He wondered if he would ever again inhale the scent of the tears of the sea.

At Lucia Luna's window he paused. He put his mouth to the slats and, with one hand resting on the machete, hoping to absorb some strength from the steel, he whispered, "I am leaving now, mi amor. Allow me two days there and two days to return. I won't fail you, I promise."

He held his breath and waited then, he listened for her response. Somebody inside the house was snoring loudly, a serrated rumble he attributed to Lucia's father. Those more delicate snores were surely her own, for they were not even snores really but only glutinous inhalations, barely louder than a cat's purr.

"Sleep sweetly, my beauty," Alberto said. He placed a kiss on his fingertips, then deposited the kiss on a shutter slat. "I leave with you my heart."

Half a minute later he turned to face the jungle, its tangle of damp leaves almost black in the half-light. Where his heart had been there was now only a fast-paced throbbing not unlike the pulse of a toothache. He freed the machete from its thong and held it up in front of him. Its wide flat blade seemed the morning's only brightness as he waded into the gloom.

"I have often wondered," the boy says, "if I would have had the courage to make such a long journey."

"Love is its own courage, nieto. Its own foolishness, and its own misfortune." The old man sighs. "Besides, your day for courage will be coming any day now. As far as I know, maybe it's already here."

"It's not the jungle that frightens me," the boy says.

"And why should it? It's crisscrossed with roads and airstrips nowadays. You couldn't walk three miles without bumping into a bulldozer. No, chico; your jungle won't be the same as mine."

He wiggles his toes in the air-conditioned sneakers. "Too bad I didn't have these shoes sixty years ago," he says. "I could have made better time."

"That Peace Corps teacher who was here last summer said that the faster a person moves, the faster time moves too. If that's true, then it wouldn't have done you any good to race through the jungle in new sneakers, because time would have been racing right along beside you."

"Milagro!" says the old man, and tries to puzzle out the implications of such a world.

"Or do I have it backwards?" the boy wonders aloud. "Maybe he said that the faster we move, the *slower* time crawls."

"Either way, it gives me a headache."

"Let's see," says the boy. "According to the first theory, if you had run faster, you would have lost time, or at least not gained any. According to the second theory, you might have gained some advantage."

"How fast would I have had to run in order to return before I left?"

"Is that possible?" the boy asks.

"Let's say I ran so fast that I left on Monday and returned from my four-day trip on Tuesday. But for Lucia Luna, who barely moved at all while I was gone, it was Thursday. On what day would we meet?"

"I'm getting dizzy," the boy says.

"I wonder . . . have I been two days behind her all these years?"

"Maybe that's what's wrong with people today. Maybe we're all living in different times, and that's why everything seems so jumbled and confused, and nobody understands what anybody else is saying or doing."

"Except for you and me, hijo. We understand each other perfectly."

"Which wouldn't be possible, I guess, if my theory were correct."

"On the other hand," the old man says, "I have often had the feeling that you *are* me, when I was younger. Or I'm an older you. I keep telling you the story to prepare you for what will happen, so that, with luck, it won't need to happen at all."

"If that's the case, how did we two get to be in the same place at the same time?"

"Maybe one of us ran so fast that we caught up with the other one going in the opposite direction."

"Or maybe one of us is dreaming."

"Or maybe somebody else is dreaming us."

The boy rubs his eyes as if dazed. Then he grins. "When all else fails," he says, " we can fall back on what the French philosopher said. 'I think, therefore I am.'"

"Unless," the grandfather counters, "we only think we think because somebody else is thinking us that way."

The boy smiles softly and gazes across the water. If he doesn't acknowledge directions, the sun can be viewed as either rising or setting. Or maybe, he reasons, it never moves at all but constantly hangs there half submerged, a brilliant orange buoy…or maybe it is a luminescent jellyfish, its long tentacles dangling. Maybe there is no such thing as time at all; there is only a single moment of existence, with all past and future nothing but the elaborate fantasy of a mind unreconciled to its brief flash of life.

Whatever the explanation, he tells himself, whether fantasy or not, one is forced to proceed under the assumption that yesterday once existed, and tomorrow probably will. "I wonder what Ernesto and Luis are doing up on the yacht right now," he says.

"Probably eating hot dogs and getting drunk."

The boy says nothing for a few moments. Then, still staring at the horizon, he remarks, "A couple of weeks ago, Ernesto went out to one of the boats and let a man take pictures of him. The man gave him a Timex, but Ernesto's afraid to wear it now because he knows his mother will ask too many questions."

The old man closes his eyes and inhales very slowly. He breathes out through his mouth then, trying to blow out some of the bruising heaviness in his chest.

After a while he opens his eyes and looks again at the boy, who seems to him very young now, a slender child, almost fragile. The old man lays a hand on the boy's shoulder, he puts two fingers against the back of the boy's neck and touches the soft black hair.

"Now that I've had a minute to consider your theories," the grandfather tells him, "I think the thing to do is to run very fast."

"Sí?" says the boy.

"But you have to run in the opposite direction than the world is spinning. That way, your speed will be doubled. And you'll cover more ground."

"But where should I be running to?" the boy asks.

"You run until you can't run anymore, nieto. Or until you don't have to. Whichever comes first."

———

Alberto ran along the sinuous path, hacking at vines and branches until his arm grew too weary to swing the blade. Not long after that, the path dissolved in a small grove of banana palms. Here some sunlight streamed through the canopy, and the air was fresher here, the greens and reds and yellows of the jungle brighter. He sat in the middle of the grove and with a round stone wearily sharpened his machete for whatever lay ahead.

He knew that the longer he sat there the more difficult it would be to get up again and push forward, so with every long grating slide of his blade across stone he imagined his resolve being sharpened too, his strength whetted. It was a kind of self-hypnotism, and it might have worked if only his stomach had cooperated. Strangely, he now found himself hungry for the first time in weeks. In fact he was ravenous. Each time he looked away from his work he saw himself gorging on bananas, or pulling a cluster of cassava roots from the black soil, or filling his pockets with nuts ... only to return home fat and sated, indifferent to love.

It was an evil temptation and it took a great force of will to limit himself to a freshening of his mouth. In the cup of a bright orange flower lay a half-inch of water, and it was with this he revitalized himself, after first picking from the liquid a beetle the size of his thumbnail, its carapace the brightest blue he had ever seen, its folded wings streaked with yellow.

He held the flower to his lips and tilted it up. Over one of the petals, curved like the side of a fluted chalice, sweet water trickled into his mouth. The sensation was dizzying. The fragrance of the just-plucked bloom mixed with the liquid warmth on his tongue. He would not allow himself to swallow, but he sloshed the water all through his mouth before finally, reluctantly, expelling it. And then he felt ashamed. "You've been walking two hours at the most," he scolded himself, "and here you are giving in already. What kind of a hero are you?" With self-castigation he thrust himself onward. With every angry swing of his blade he tried to slice away his fear and his doubt.

And yet, the jungle was everywhere. Thorny vines wrapped around his ankles and conspired to pull him down. Branches whipped at his face, cutting his cheeks. Insects stung, leaves rustled, bushes made ominous rattling sounds. There was no sky, only a black interlacing of leaves.

No sun, only bug-filled bars of light that tilted and broke as the day wore on.

"Not long into that first afternoon," the old man remembers, "I figured I was done for. The canopy seemed to be pushing down on my head, and although the ground was solid, I felt as if I were wading through swamp. Once, when my fatigue had made me careless, I let go of a branch too quickly. It snapped back and slashed across my forehead, hitting me so hard that I fell down. Sitting there in the dirt, I realized then that I had bitten off more than I could chew. All I wanted was to go to sleep and never wake up."

Alberto lay back against the cool earth. He let his heels scrape across the ground, his legs stretching out. He closed his eyes and waited for the black ceiling of leaves and branches to fall down and crush him.

After a while, the knot in his stomach loosened. His breathing came regularly again, and the twitterings and squawks of the jungle faded into the distance. He felt himself drifting toward a pale yellow glade of sleep.

"Por amor, Alberto," he heard whispered in his left ear, the voice as clear and resonant as if Lucia's lips were but half an inch away. "Vivir y morir por amor…"

He sat bolt upright, eyes wide open. The jungle was silent, unmoving. Then there was a flash of yellow off to his right as a bird fluttered to another limb. "Por amor!" a parrot squawked from behind the leaves. "Por amor, querido, por amor, por amor!"

Alberto dug his fingernails into the soft earth and pried loose a rock. Then he leapt to his feet and heaved the rock high into the tree. "Shut up!" he screamed. ""You hear me? Shut up or I will climb up there and cut you in half!"

He waited, breathless, but there was no answer. The jungle said nothing. A moment later, Alberto was unsure if he had actually thrown a rock or not, if he had actually heard the parrot taunt him or merely dreamed it. He laughed softly at himself.

"But at least I was on my feet again," the old man says. "And so, I decided to keep going."

His resolve did not last long. Each step was harder than the one before, each vine thicker, sharper, more difficult to cut. And following behind him, on his right and then on his left, came the high-pitched squawk of "Por amor, pimiento! Don't forget—por amor!"

Soon it was easier to keep moving than to stop. But he no longer knew or cared where he was headed, whether he was awake or dreaming, alive or already dead. His machete dragged on the ground, dangling from his wrist by its leather thong. Dizziness came and went in quick cold waves, and there was a bitter taste in his mouth.

More than once he thought he saw the blue and yellow beetle crawling up his arm, but when he moved to flick it away, he saw only a fleck of rotted leaf, a particle of dirt. Miles later, when his foot caught in a root and he pitched forward onto his hands and knees, he did not resent the fall but was grateful for the root's intervention, and without attempting to rise he lay prostrate on the ground, his cheek to the earth, his mind empty of any thought but resignation . . .

Alberto felt the ground rumbling beneath him, he heard a thundering of earth in his ear. At first his eyelids felt as if they had been glued shut, but with effort and increasing alarm as the thundering escalated, he managed finally to open them, only to behold a jungle lit entirely in various shades of red. The tree trunks were crimson, the ferns maroon. Vines were the color of new blood. Grasses were carnation or cinnabar or vermilion. Ribbons of sunlight were pink. And even as he pushed himself to his knees, even as he then tried to rub the redness from his eyes, the thundering grew louder. Soon it was accompanied by a crackling of bushes, a snapping of twigs.

The thought that he should leap to his feet and run occurred to Alberto just an instant before the wild boar came crashing through the brush, its huge black head lowered, tusks and long pink snout nearly scraping the ground.

Alberto had no time to move; he merely thrust his hands out in front of himself, but felt them slip harmlessly along the sides of the beast, its gray skin not bristly and rough but smooth to the touch, as cool as shaded stone. A moment later the crown of the animal's skull rammed into Alberto's stomach and he went sailing backward through the air, red leaves whipping past him until he dropped to the ground again in a tangle of writhing ferns.

"For a moment I just lay there very still with my face in the grass," the old man explains. "My first thought was one of surprise that I was still conscious. I waited for the pain to come and tell me what was broken. But there was no pain, and the wind that had been punched from my lungs quickly returned. I lay there amazed that I was still in one piece, and, unless I had been knocked clear into the next life, none the worse for it."

But then came a snorted grunt, and in a flash Alberto rolled over and leapt to his feet, prepared to grab the nearest tree limb and hoist himself to safety. His arms never rose above his chest, however; he froze. For standing there before him, surrounded by a jungle no longer stained red but colored in soft, shimmering blues and pale yellows, was Arcadio Martín in his immaculate white suit.

Without actually lifting the porkpie hat from his head, Martín bowed slightly and tipped his hat toward Alberto. "You are a long way from home, fisherman," he said.

Alberto could only stare. Half a minute passed before he rediscovered his voice. "I am engaged in a mission," he stammered.

"Ah, una misión de amor. So it is you the jungle has been squawking about." Arcadio Martín smiled. "And what is the nature of your mission, hombre? Have you come, perhaps, to kill a jaguar?"

Alberto's hand went to his machete then, but he found only the broken leather thong still attached to his wrist. Quickly he looked to the ground, then behind him, where he had fallen. But there was no sign of his knife. When he returned to his original position a moment later, he saw Arcadio Martín flipping the machete end over end, deftly catching it by the handle.

"Were you planning to fillet me, señor?" Martín asked.

Unarmed, defenseless, Alberto puffed out his chest. "I will do whatever is necessary. Or I will die trying."

Martín nodded slightly, impressed. He held the machete motionless then. He regarded the blade. "There are at least two outsides and one inside to everything," he told the boy. "And every inside is itself two outsides. And so ... is there perhaps some side to this situation that you would like to ask me about?"

Until that moment, Alberto had been unaware of any questions. But suddenly a great sadness welled up inside him. He felt it growing from somewhere below his stomach and up into his chest, a warm and heavy blossoming of sadness that expanded into his throat and formed itself in words ... words as hoarse and dry as failure.

"Did you really make love to her?" he asked.

Arcadio Martín shrugged. "For a thing to grow, a seed must be planted, no?"

Reluctantly, bitterly, Alberto nodded.

"On the other hand," said Martín, "perhaps a bird dropped the seed from the sky. Perhaps the wind blew it over from Africa. Perhaps it was a seed of thought she swallowed, or a seed of her own imagination. Or perhaps," and now he smiled again, a wan smile, thin-lipped and tired, "perhaps it was one from the showers of seeds that so often burst from your guitar."

He shrugged again, then flipped the machete away. It stuck in the ground at Alberto's feet, the blade quivering. Alberto looked at it for a moment, then reached down and freed it from the earth. But he held the blade flat against his leg.

"*Are* you a devil?" Alberto asked. "Or are you only a dolphin-man?"

"Which would you like me to be?"

Alberto did not answer. Now that he had opened his heart to questions, there seemed no end to them. "Am I wrong for loving her?"

"Do you think you are?"

Alberto did not know what he thought. Anger and grief swirled through him, resentment and sorrow. He looked away from Martín and tried to find some certainty in the blue of the jungle, but the only sureness that came to him was of the beauty of this strange world. It was as if a summer sky had been sculpted into trees and bushes and vines and grass; the blinding gold of the sun hammered into leaves and fruit so thin as to be translucent.

When he faced Arcadio Martín again, Alberto was no longer angry. He said, "I think the only thing we can trust in this life is the music and mystery of the heart."

Arcadio Martín smiled. Touching his fingertips to the brim of his hat, he bowed deeply. Without rising, he backed away into the brush.

"Wait!" Alberto called. "Will I find you in Nuevas Alijas, señor?"

The answer came from behind a curtain of leaves that no longer rustled. "You have found me already, guerrero."

Alberto waited for more, but there were no other sounds—no words, no fading footsteps. He had many more questions, but they could be postponed, he told himself, until tomorrow afternoon when he reached Nuevas Alijas. For now, this was a good place to spend the night. The colors were deepening, the blues settling into an indigo twilight, the yellows into orchid. Alberto knew he would be safe here; he no longer felt afraid.

Filled with a quiet exuberance, an optimism he could not explain, Alberto peered into the treetops. He drew back his arm and hurled the machete end over end. Just before it sailed into the branches he thought he saw the long blade open its wings and become a silver seagull. He felt better for having released it. It would find its way back to the shore soon, and, in three more days, so would he.

The night came swiftly and filled all spaces. Alberto slept for a few hours, then awoke to find himself engulfed in the profoundest darkness he had ever experienced. The night was absolute. Yet Alberto did not feel boxed in by it, he felt protected—ensconced. A pair of green eyes peered down at him from twenty feet up in the blackness, but Alberto's heartbeat remained steady and calm. He knew that his eyes were green too; that he was either the seer or the seer's reflection. In either case, he was looking at himself.

"The night changed you," the boy says, "didn't it, grandfather?"

And the old man nods. "That is the way it is with surrender."

Alberto awoke to a jungle steaming with life, awash in brilliant but natural colors, clamorous with the caws and squawks and chitterings of a routine morning. A moment after his eyes fluttered open, a moth as big as a butterfly lifted off the tip of his nose where it had been drying its wings in a shaft of light, broad dusty white wings with two yellow moons, one large and one small, on each surface.

Alberto lay very still and watched the moth in flight, hoping it would return to its perch. Instead it spiraled higher and higher, in and out of the sunlight, until it escaped through the branches and into open sky.

Alberto sat up. Between his legs, its neck craned upward, bulging eyes staring, sat an iguana. Apparently it had been eyeing the moth, maneuvering into position for breakfast.

"Buenos días," Alberto said. The lizard flicked its tongue at him. Then it turned its head slightly, froze for a moment, and flicked its long tongue at a mosquito on Alberto's trousers.

Laughing softly, Alberto rolled onto his side, then climbed to his feet. He reached as high as he could, grabbed two handfuls of air and pulled himself onto his toes, stretching. He felt strong this morning, reassured by his dreams of the previous night.

He spent nearly an hour climbing a tree so as to stand finally at the very top of the jungle canopy, waist-high in an ocean of green. From this vantage point he could see the sun on one horizon and a pale white moon on the other. Between the two, hugging a thin strip of seacoast, were the chalky low buildings of Nuevas Alijas. Alberto could not restrain himself from indulging in a whoop of victory, a high shrill cry of delight that brought thousands of birds bursting into the sky all around him, a whirring cloud of wings.

Minutes later he climbed down again. A long day's walk remained ahead of him, but he was not dismayed. He knew that he had only to keep moving, one foot in front of the other, until he could smell the ocean, and then to walk a few miles more. His clothes were torn and dirty, his arms and face streaked with bloody scratches, but this was of no concern to him. He felt as if he had defeated something wild and strong, though he could not have described it or given it a name.

"In those days," the old man recounts, "there were still lots of people who believed that plants and trees can think. And the more I walked, the more I believed it too. Those plants were giving me the once-over, maybe even letting each other know I was on my way. They're poker-faced, every last one of them, but they're good at sizing people up. Not that I was disturbed by their attention, you understand. It was only natural that they should want to keep an eye on me. Besides, I came to understand that they didn't mean me any harm. When a vine sneaked out to grab my ankle and yank me down, for example, or when a branch snapped its leaves in my face, they were just being playful. The smaller plants, especially, are a lot like children.

"And so," the old man says, "through the remainder of that morning and afternoon I marched. I no longer felt the mosquitoes gnawing on me; they had already numbed my skin with their bites. Inside and outside myself I marched, my body stumbling on mechanically, growing fatigued again and hurting in every joint, while my mind drifted effortlessly through the branches, as agile as a serpent.

"Everything I experienced had two meanings for me. On the ground I was startled by the sudden shrieks of birds and the growls and grunts from the bushes, but that part of me gliding through the trees heard only harmony in those cries, and I knew that even if the beasts tore me limb from limb, it would not really matter. I knew I had been assigned a duty and that I must complete it, but at the same time I sensed it was all a play of some kind, una ópera bufa, to which I was both the audience and the clown."

Late in the afternoon Alberto emerged from the jungle and stepped into a clearing. Here, on a swath of land nearly one hundred feet wide, all the foliage had been stripped away in preparation for another row of buildings. Terraced below this clearing, leading down to the coastline some two hundred yards away, lay Nuevas Alijas.

With his first glimpse of the town Alberto stopped in his tracks and gaped. Compared to Mundosuave, Nuevas Alijas was huge. Here the people lived not in wooden shacks but in houses of stone or red clay or whitewashed adobe, with roofs of red tile or sheets of rippled tin. There were thousands of people down there in the streets, coming and going, attending to business.

He counted a half dozen ships in the harbor, and three times as many smaller boats moored to a pier that stuck into the ocean like the city's tongue, lapping up its riches. A few automobiles, the first he had ever seen, chugged along the unpaved streets, horns bleating, drivers screaming at pedestrians and animals in their path. All in all it was a dizzying sight, at once more terrifying and exciting than the jungle. And the ocean beyond ... so blue it was; so sun-speckled and bright!

With a step more suited to the damp softness of the jungle floor than to dirt streets scraped bare and trampled hard, Alberto moved toward the center of town, toward the wide and bustling market square he had glimpsed from above. So intrigued was he by his surroundings that he gave no thought to his own appearance or to the stares and whispers it elicited from the citizens he passed along the way, citizens who gawked wide-eyed until he came too near, then hurriedly crossed the street or pulled their children from his path or rushed into the safety of the nearest doorway.

To these people, accustomed to the quick shuffling gait of commerce, Alberto appeared to move with a fluidity more natural to the animal or spirit world. His feet, like a stalking cat's, barely seemed to touch the ground. His skin was black with ticks and bloody scratches, his clothes caked with dried mud, his hair matted with leaves. Down the center of the street he walked toward the cluster of vendors in the middle of the square, his head turning slowly from side to side, trying to take it all in, the noise and activity, the smells of food and cut flowers and the narcotic stink of too much humanity rubbing up against itself. So entranced was he by it all that he forgot to blink. Even grown men shrank away from him.

"Where did *that* come from?" a woman whispered.

"The jungle. Didn't you see?"

"Not from our jungle, he didn't."

"Look at his eyes," said a man with a small child on his shoulders. "Those aren't human eyes."

"Don't let them fall on you!"

Alberto heard the buzz and hum of their voices; he looked their way and smiled.

"Did you see that? He snarled at me!"

An attractive young maid, on her way home with a fresh mackerel for her employer's evening meal, shifted her basket to the other hand and made the sign of the cross.

"I tell you he isn't human. Look at those eyes. He's half wolf."

"Three-quarters wolf, if you ask me."

Alberto came to a halt in front of a fruit stall. Oblivious to the small crowd that had formed behind him, he looked straight at the vendor and smiled. The vendor, a thin man with a pockmarked face, took a step backward. Then he reached forward, quickly chose his brightest apple, and with a trembling hand offered it to Alberto.

"I have no need for food," Alberto told him.

A murmur of awe, of suspicions confirmed, rippled through the crowd. The noise prompted Alberto to face them; en masse, they retreated three steps.

"I have come for Arcadio Martín," he announced.

Again the crowd murmured. They put their heads together and whispered. "Lo siento," said the apple vendor. "But there is no one by that name in this town."

"I know that there is," said Alberto, "for I spoke with his doble in the jungle."

This time the crowd did not murmur, but gasped.

"I know of no one by that name," the vendor reiterated. "Es verdad, lobato, I swear."

A second vendor stood by the first. "We have an Arcadio Sanchez, wolfboy. And Arcadio Gomez. We have Emilio Martín, Eligio Martín, Ruperto and Carmelio Martín. Would you care to eat one of them instead?"

"Arcadio Martín is a tall man," said Alberto, "and very thin. He wears a white suit and a straw porkpie hat. It is a comical little hat with a bright yellow band. Martín does not take his hand off this hat even when he dances."

"He is talking about a dolphin-man!" a woman exclaimed.

A man from the crowd spoke up. "What does a wolfboy want with a dolphin-man?"

Their confusion amused Alberto. He could not help smiling at them. Unfortunately, with his dirt and blood-streaked face, and with his body reeking of the dark scent of the jungle, his smile appeared more sinister than sweet.

A big man at the rear of the crowd, his shoulders as broad as those of Alberto's friend Poco, said, "The only dolphin-man we have ever seen wore a tricornio pulled low over his eyes. Could this be the one you seek?"

"What did he look like?" Alberto asked.

"Short, like an Indian. And very dark."

"He was not a good dancer," a woman added.

"His teeth were bad," said another. "Whew, I can still smell that breath!"

"And as for not using both hands," a third woman said, "this one certainly did!"

Several people in the crowd chuckled, but Alberto shook his head. "That was not Arcadio Martín."

"Then go away, why don't you? There's nothing for you here."

Alberto's somber expression prompted a minute of silence. He pivoted slowly, allowing his gaze to sweep across the crowded square. For some reason the place looked less attractive to him now, less exciting. Maybe it was because the sun was going down, slanting in low over the ocean. Across the square several vendors were hurriedly packing up, closing their stalls, preparing to drag their carts home. The ground, now that Alberto noticed it, was littered with pieces of half-eaten food, rotten fruit, crumpled sheets of soiled newspaper. Flies buzzed everywhere, filling the air with an annoying hum.

Alberto felt a tap on his shoulder then. He turned back to the crowd. There stood a butcher in his bloody apron, two newly-killed chickens in his right hand, their necks limp, eyes glassy, wings jerking as if trying to remember how to fly. The down of other chickens still stuck to the man's greasy forearms, with a few tiny feathers clinging to his sweaty cheeks as well.

Bowing deeply, the butcher laid his offering at Alberto's feet, and backed away. The birds' muscles continued to twitch, discharging their last energies.

Alberto stared in disgust at the chickens. Suddenly he felt nauseated—sick of himself for believing, like a child, that all he would have to do was to ask, then waltz Arcadio Martín back to Mundosuave, then live with his love in eternal happiness; sick with the suspicion that he was being played for a fool. "If you are attempting to hide him from me...," he muttered.

"We have no Arcadio Martín," a man quickly replied. "His spirit deceived you."

"We're not to blame."

"You can't hold us responsible."

"Take your chickens and leave us, malvado. You have no right coming here."

"You're driving away the day's last customers."

"This is no place for a thing like you."

"We're not helpless, you know. Our police are well armed."

"Somebody send for the police, quick!"

"And the dog catcher! Hurry!"

To Alberto their words were like the buzzing of fat flies. He lifted his head and gazed out across the ocean. His weariness returned in a rush. Every muscle and joint in his body suddenly ached anew. He felt like lying down right there in the dirt, curling up in a ball, an armadillo of defeat, and letting the flies devour him...

One of the dead chickens flopped six inches in the air, did a somersault and landed atop his foot, its wing flapping wildly. Alberto backed away, slowly retreating until he bumped into the fruit stall, which brought a small cascade of apples tumbling down. He turned abruptly and swung out his arm, though no one dared block his path. In a daze he began retracing his steps, but erratically this time, veering from left to right and back again.

He walked for twenty yards before the butcher caught up with him. Thrusting the pair of chickens against Alberto's chest, the man said, "Your dinner, wolfboy. Here, take them with you, compliments of el carnicero Lebredo—"

Alberto's face went taut, his eyes black. Seizing one chicken in each hand he tore them from the startled butcher's grasp and, spinning in a half-circle, flung them high into the air, simultaneously screaming, his anger and frustration exploding in a shrill and prolonged, "Aiiiieeeeee!"

Everyone in the square ducked or dove or fled for cover.

One chicken and then the other finally thudded to the ground. Immediately, from beneath a nearby stall, a scrawny dog streaked out to seize one of the birds. It locked its jaws around the chicken's neck and then whipped the limp body back and forth, dislodging feathers, kicking up dust. Then, satisfied that there would be no resistance, the dog trotted away with its prize, the chicken's feet scratching broken lines in the dirt.

Alberto trudged back uphill, fists clenched. Now and then a fluffy pin feather floated away from him.

With his back to the jungle he sat on the ground, glaring down at Nuevas Alijas. He did not know whether to blame the town or Arcadio Martín for his failure. He hated them both.

As for Martín—what kind of creature was he? Dolphin-man, spirit, hallucination, or just a peddler of lies, a merchant of phony names and addresses? Had his porkpie hat concealed a blowhole or only a bald spot?

And what was Alberto to tell Lucia Luna now? What hope could he offer? Maybe the thing to do was to sneak back to Mundosuave and rescue his love from the town's hysteria; spirit her away to safety.

But to where—where could they go?

Certainly not to Nuevas Alijas. Even from so far above the city he could smell its stink of ill will and avarice. It smelled worse than a wet goat, worse than a spoiled fish. Not even the occasional ocean breeze could freshen it. He could see the townspeople stopping from time to time to stare up at him and point. Now and then somebody shook a fist at him, or threw a stone that fell a hundred yards short.

Alberto sat there trying to will an earthquake to shiver up from the center of the earth and crack Nuevas Alijas down the middle, crumble its buildings, stir up a tidal wave to flush the coastline clean. He thought so long and hard that as twilight descended he found his anger fading with the light, expiated, his desire for revenge supplanted by a simpler desire to merely separate himself from this place, to erase it with distance.

Stiffly he stood, eager for the jungle. It was then he saw the enormous fireflies bobbing along a side street, at least a dozen of them weaving from one building to another in single file, coming closer. But these fireflies smelled like burning tar, and they dripped eggs of flaming pitch onto the streets, and they streamed long tails of black smoke.

At the end of town the men carrying these torches closed ranks as they passed the final building. They formed a crude half-circle, convex, approaching haltingly, murmuring now, each man attempting to conceal his fear by encouraging the others forward.

Step by step Alberto backed toward the jungle. He could see the men's faces now—fearful frowning masks illuminated by the flickering orange glow. A few of the men carried rifles.

In desperation he took a final look at the ocean, so blue-black and calm. He cupped his hands to his mouth and released an anguished cry, *"Arcadio Martin!"* The name echoed again and again, but he received no answer.

At the sound of Alberto's scream, four men dropped their torches and fled back into town. Three others soon decided to join them. But the remaining men stood their ground. Bit by bit they advanced on the treeline, rifles at the ready.

Alberto turned and ran into the darkness. With his first breath of damp air he felt better, surer of his step even though the way was dim, safer though surrounded by the invisible and unknown. But in a matter of minutes his path grew brighter, and with a glance over his shoulder he saw the world ablaze behind him, the jungle afire now, crackling and hissing, a strange high wall of gray-green smoke chasing after him, leaping forward on legs of orange and blue and gold. The men from Nuevas Alijas had set the jungle on fire, hoping to reduce Alberto to ashes. Headlong Alberto ran, with no direction other than away from the flames. When uncertain of which way to go, he followed the birds as they flapped and squawked above. He ran until the fire seemed inside as well as outside him, scorching his lungs, burning his joints and muscles. He ran backwards through time, through a jungle night that became twilight, then afternoon, then as bright and dry and searing as midday. He ran past fear and beyond exhaustion, he ran well into indifference. And when he could run no more he slowed, he walked, he stopped. He turned to face the wall and to let it overtake him.

Ten yards away stood a jaguar, its green eyes bright. For fifteen seconds Alberto did not move, and neither did the cat.

"It was a strange situation," the old man says. "There I was, willing to be burned to death in order to have a rest from this struggle, and what do I come face-to-face with but a different kind of danger. And to be honest, nieto, this one did not appeal to me quite as much. Maybe I just hadn't had enough time to get used to the idea of a mauling, I don't know. In any case, I took a good long look at the cat's jaws, and I started moving again."

Cautiously Alberto tried a backward step. Then another... another. The jaguar did not spring forward, did not sink into its pounce. It kept apace, moving forward as Alberto did.

"And not in its stalking posture either, that was the strange part. Once, when I tripped and fell down on my behind, I thought that was the end of it, I was dinner for sure. But the cat just stood there and waited, coming no closer. It even seemed to be grinning at me—though it's hard to say whether that was so or not; cats have a highly developed sense of humor, and, unlike humans, they are seldom amused by misfortune."

Finally Alberto climbed to his feet and, so as to increase his pace, faced forward again. Every second or so he took another glance over his shoulder. The jaguar never came any closer nor fell further back.

"I started to trot then, and the cat trotted too. It was an easy pace now that I had my breath back, and, because I was now convinced that he had no intention of eating me, an enjoyable one. I began to sense the rhythm of his movement, the padded fall of his footsteps, and this became my rhythm too. I was soon loping along as easily as a cat myself."

It wasn't long before Alberto felt a breeze cooling his face, and he became aware of the leaves stirring all around him. A moment later the rain began, one of those sudden downpours that, in a clearing, would fall bruising and fierce, but through the jungle canopy it descended as a melodious shower. Behind him the ground hissed and the flames flickered and dimmed. Alberto slowed his pace and looked over his shoulder less frequently. He knew the cat was still there, as was the rain, and the charred remains of his fear.

He walked on another hour or so, deeper into the night, the warm rain washing him clean. Finally he came to a thick-bellied tree whose roots lay atop the ground in a wide U-shape, and inside this niche the ground was dry, protected by the curving trunk itself. It seemed a natural thing for him to curl up inside these roots and rest. He fell asleep gazing into the branches, peering up at a forked limb fifteen feet overhead, nothing visible but the pair of watchful green eyes, nothing audible but the patter of inspiriting rain.

"This is one of the parts I like best," the boy says.

"And why is that, nieto?"

"Everything is good in this part. Nobody gets hurt here."

"An interlude," the old man says.

"That first moment in the morning when you awoke," the boy prompts, "and you found yourself stretched out in the fork of the branches, looking down at the jaguar curled up between the tree roots, as if the two of you had switched positions in the night... tell me again what it was you thought."

"I thought, 'Move softly; you don't want to frighten him.'"

"It was the cat's thought," the boy says, "thinking inside your head."

"That was my initial impression, yes. And for a moment I didn't know whether I was man or cat or something in between. But my confusion lasted only a few seconds, and then, when I realized my situation, I knew nothing but alarm. Last night's serenity seemed little more than a Lady of the Night, that bush whose flowers open up in the darkness and give off a seductive scent, only to wilt and close at first light. I didn't even waste any time wondering how the cat and I had changed beds. What bothered me now was how I was going to get past him without waking him up. Everybody knows that cats wake up hungry because their dreams smell like little birds."

With excruciating slowness Alberto crawled further out on his limb. Each time the limb creaked under his weight, he froze in place and held his breath. The cat never stirred.

Finally Alberto could advance no farther lest the limb snap. With every muscle tensed, he let his legs dangle. Inch by inch he allowed his arms to straighten as he hung from the branch with both hands. With his shoes still nine and a half feet above the ground, he let himself drop.

"Even before I hit the ground," the old man remembers, "that cat was on its feet. It woke up licking its lips. So I turned in mid-air, making sure I landed with my back to him. My own feet had barely kissed the earth before I was in motion, flying through the brush, trying to see through the blur of green some way to save myself from his teeth."

"Maybe you should have stayed in the tree until the cat woke up and wandered off," the boy suggests.

"Why would he have wandered off when he knew exactly where I was?"

"Maybe," the boy concedes. "But on the other hand—"

"On the other hand, nieto, this would be a different story had I not done precisely as I did. This story, in fact, would not exist. This story depends on my getting down out of the tree, whether it was rational to do so or not. In this story, as in life itself, everything is connected. Don't let's start shifting the puzzle pieces around at this point. The past can't be revised."

"Unless, as you said earlier, it only exists as a memory we create as we go along."

The old man sighs. He smiles good-naturedly. "It's natural for you to be so curious," he says. "It's good for a boy your age to question things. Question everything, nieto; always expect more than you are told; anticipate more than you can see. And always dream of more than you are given. If you are not dissatisfied and a little bit skeptical, nothing will ever change.

"As for me and my story, however, I wish you would quit being so contentious."

"You seem especially tired today, grandfather."

"Maybe that's all it is."

"I'll try not to interrupt again."

"And I'll try to be more patient when you fail."

Within minutes of breaking into his panicked run, Alberto lost all sense of direction. He could hear nothing but his own movement, his gasping breath and the slash and rustle of leaves. He was certain that at any moment he would be knocked down from behind, and a second later feel a mouthful of teeth clamping onto his neck.

Instead, he felt a slap of cooler, brighter air in his face, he felt the world pulled out from beneath him, and he felt his stomach soaring into his throat as he crashed through the treeline and plummeted over an embankment. He fell only six or eight feet, but then slid another twenty on his back before coming to rest in thick grass. He could hear and smell the ocean not far away, could see a mother-of-pearl sky overhead.

Incredulous, Alberto sat up. All around him was verdant meadow, wide and long and dotted with wildflowers. The meadow gave way eventually to a strip of sandy beach curving around a natural harbor, a gravel bar extending into the sea to form the breakwater of an azure lagoon. A hundred yards upshore a stream gushed out of the jungle to cascade over the embankment and into another streambed, which, when it reached the sand, spread out sparkling and fanlike over the beach.

Already oblivious to his pain, Alberto stood. Bruised and bleeding, his shirt torn, back lacerated, he grinned broadly. Wanting to take in the full panorama of this paradise, he slowly turned to face the jungle again, and there saw the jaguar looking down on him from the edge of the embankment, smiling as cats do.

Suddenly Alberto understood that the jaguar had not been pursuing him at all; it had been chasing him to this very spot, leading him from behind. "Muchas gracias," Alberto called. "You will be welcome here anytime."

With those words, a wonderful plan sprang into his head. "The house will be there," he said, pointing upshore, "so that we can bathe in the stream. With a garden here. And down there is where I will throw my net, without any rocks to tear it or cut my feet!"

Overcome with joy, he spread his arms to the ocean. "All will be welcome here!" he called. "All is forgiven!"

With renewed strength, he strode toward the waterfall. Once there he set to work wrestling stones from the streambed, large round foundation stones that he piled one atop another, laying out the corners of his walls, talking incessantly.

"Every night I will play my guitar and Lucia Luna will sing. The dolphins will come ashore to dance and the jaguars to listen. We will learn to speak each other's language—eh, gato?" He looked toward the jungle again and, aburst with optimism, he roared.

"Our child will thrive here—the first of many children! Here between the wild and the sea. An amphibious child—mestizo! A child favored by heaven and earth...a return to the way we used to be!"

Nearly delirious with hope and goodwill, Alberto continued to work throughout the day, sometimes bursting into song, sometimes talking, tirelessly building, crazy with joy.

The boy says, "I always wish this were the end of it, grandfather. Wouldn't this make the perfect place to stop?"

The old man clears his throat and swallows something hard. "It is a lovely madness, sí."

~~~~~~

Alberto awakened to a new day in the half-finished doorway of his stone hut. The sun was already shining over the low walls, which rose no higher than his waist on all four sides. He could not remember a morning so beautiful as this one, a light so golden and sweet. He knew that his life was changed now, that the pendulum had swung from misfortune to triumph. His head was clear and he knew exactly what he must do. He would march into Mundosuave by late afternoon, commandeer a donkey, and escort Lucia Luna back to this place where tragedy did not exist. No one would dare enjoin him.

Because all would soon be corrected, all negatives cancelled out, he decided to allow himself a sip of water from the stream. It seemed the natural thing to do, a good thing, the end of self-denial, a gesture of reward. He lay on his belly on the grassy bank and lowered his mouth to the water. For a moment he thought he might faint from the cold delicious shock of it, the sudden sensation of falling, of plummeting through darkness. The water was sweet, dizzying, addictive; he could not stop with a sip but gulped so thirstily that he began to cough and had to pull away finally and sit up. His belly felt heavy then; too full.

Even so, he would not let his optimism fade. He looked back toward the hut, and grinned proudly. "When I return with my bride," he announced, "I will finish the walls and put on a roof. No man could have done better."

With that he stood and faced the opposite direction. He glanced over his shoulder at the rising sun. "Are you ready?" he asked it. Then, "Go!" Sprinting hard, he raced upshore, angling toward the jungle, his heavy belly sloshing.

The old man pauses now, bent almost double over his useless guitar. He remains in this posture for so long that the boy wonders if he has fallen asleep, or worse. He is afraid to touch the old man's shoulder, afraid of the coldness he might feel, but he forces himself to do so. The old man's body is warm, but for half a minute he offers no response.

"That water slowed me down," the old man finally says, a mumble into splintered wood.

"I thought you were sleeping," the boy tells him.

The old man sits up and looks him in the eye. "We are all sleeping, chico. The entire planet is fast asleep."

"Even you and me?"

"We're talking in our sleep, yes. We do everything in our sleep. Everybody does."

The boy is silent for a moment. "I guess I don't know what you mean by that."

"Then never mind." A few seconds pass, and the old man smiles softly, ashamed of his brief anger. "I don't make a lot of sense sometimes, do I?"

"It's all right," the boy tells him. Because a part of him does understand after all, though in a vague way that will not fit itself to words. He looks at the dimming sky, the darkening sea, and he thinks of the past two hours, of sitting here like a child while the light fades all around. What good has he made of the afternoon? Nothing is changed. Tomorrow will be another today; today was yesterday. Maybe it is time, as his mother says, to give up his story hour; time to act like a man. Unfortunately, he is not quite sure what that means either.

"Let's finish the story," the boy says finally.

And the old man nods. "We have to."

———

The sun seemed unbearably bright as Alberto broke briskly through the tangled brush to step into Mundosuave, the sun hanging out above the ocean now, a glaring white ball that bleached the sky of all color. In one step the ground had turned from pliant to unyielding, from comforting to hard. The air, so moist and rich with one breath, had become desiccated with the next. Only now, when these sensations hit him like a slap, did Alberto break stride from the confident pace that had carried him through the jungle.

He paused for just a moment to readjust and take his bearings. That his clothes were filthy and torn, his skin black with grime, seemed of no consequence. If anything, his appearance gave substance to the ordeal he had endured; he wore it as a badge of honor.

The position of the sun told him that midday was hours past; it was now the hottest time of the day. And so it did not strike him as unusual that the town was still, that he could discern no movement other than a few chickens and panting dogs. He had emerged from the jungle at the southern end of town, and now, as he made his way up the single dirt street, looking from one silent house to the next, he smiled to himself and imagined his neighbors rising from siesta to peer out from behind their shuttered windows, remarking to one another how brave he looked, how tall, the mere sight of him making them feel timid and small as they hid from the sun.

While still fifty yards off he fixed his gaze on the Luna house. No doubt Lucia would be disappointed at first when he told her of his experience in Nuevas Alijas, but he would talk quickly and recount his discovery of their personal Eden, of how he had been led there by a jaguar, and of how that jaguar was probably the same spirit that appeared to him in the jungle as Arcadio Martín, and of how this was all interconnected, fated, his destiny and hers two halves of the same ...

When he tapped lightly on the shutter of Lucia Luna's window, the shutter creaked open, unlocked. He whispered her name. When there was no response, he eased the shutter open wider.

Her bedroom was empty. The thin straw mattress had been split open, the serape over her doorway ripped down. Alberto felt a darkness rush out at him, a shadow so tangible that he staggered away from the window and into the center of the street.

Still no one moved, nobody spoke. There were no sounds but for the roaring in his ears. For a moment he wondered if this was truly Mundosuave. Maybe he had come out of the jungle too soon, only to wander into this ghost place, this town of black spirits and wordless deceptions.

He turned quickly toward the ocean, the one thing he trusted. And there he saw her, an old woman in a gray dress, huddled alone not far from the edge of the cliff, gazing out to sea. It could have been any of several viejas he knew. Whoever she was, she would soon tell him what was going on here.

And as he approached her, he had a startling thought: They were all off searching for him! Of course, he should have known how worried they would be. His parents would be half mad with grief by now. And Lucia Luna, who perhaps had been forced to reveal his mission, they had dragged her along!

Only this one old woman had been left behind to wait and pray, too decrepit to be of any other use. "Perdón, abuela," Alberto said. He spoke softly, and softly touched her shoulder. The old woman, a mad smile on her lips, looked up at him.

Alberto's knees buckled, and he dropped down beside her. The darkness swirled in the pit of his belly, and he had to squeeze his stomach hard so as not to be sick. "Mi amor," he muttered, "mi bella... what in the name of the mother of God...?"

Lucia Luna offered no reply. In her right hand she held a gnarled stick, with which she began scratching in the dirt. Alberto lay his hand upon her pallid cheek, he lifted her chin and brought her gaze back to his. Her eyes were as hard as agates, as black as death.

"What's going on here?" he asked.

She raised the stick and pointed out to sea. Tiny black shapes wobbled against the horizon, the town's fleet of fishing boats etched upon the sky.

"But the women," he said, and rose to his feet for a closer look, and as he came to the edge of the cliff he saw them huddled below, some staring out across the waves, some sitting on the rocks with heads bowed and buried between their knees. It was natural that the men should be fishing, but the women were gathered on the beach too early. And the way they looked ... those huddled postures. It did not seem right.

And then it came to him. "It's part of the jaguar's plan!" he said. "With everyone gone, we can sneak away unnoticed!"

He took her hand and raised it to his lips. She continued to stare at him, her lips thin and smiling, a scratch of derision.

"I have found a place for us, bella. Such beauty and peace as you could never imagine. A place for the baby to grow strong and free."

She twisted her hand in his and, squeezing his fingers, pulled his hand down to the bulge of her dress. She pressed his hand against this bulge and the dress went flat, the air forced out, and through the thin cloth Alberto felt the slackness of her stomach, the loose and empty skin.

The darkness swirled into his head then and he swooned sideways, onto his buttocks. Only by catching himself with his hand did he keep from falling over. Dizzied, gasping for breath, he again peered out to sea. And now he understood. He knew what they were doing out there, and why the women below looked so tragic. He squeezed shut his eyes, hoping for blackness, but the pictures he saw inside his head were even more horrifying—of gulls squawking and diving around the fifteen small boats, fish swarming in such a frenzy that the water seems to boil, sharks moving in from a mile away, the current spiced with the scent of blood, placenta, slippery new flesh, one of the fishermen beseeching the sea with an ancient prayer only half-remembered, *Take this offering and leave us alone ...*

Lucia Luna grinned and scratched another word in the dust. Two minutes later, as Alberto rocked back and forth, clutching his own stomach, she read what she had written there. "Maldición," she croaked, her voice as jagged as broken glass. "Muerte. Estrago…"

"Damnation," the old man rasps. "Death. And destruction."

Both he and the boy sit quietly in the gathering gloom. The old man fingers the strings of his guitar. For a long time, neither of them speaks.

Finally the boy rises and, after a moment's pause, crosses to the edge of the square. He leans against the low stone wall, he squints into the distance.

"Why don't you go join your friends now," the old man suggests. "The gringos can be very generous when they've been drinking."

"They have nothing I want," the boy says.

The old man sits motionless, staring at the ground. Three minutes pass. "I don't think I will tell you that story again, nieto."

"That's what you always say."

"This time I mean it."

"I hope you don't," the boy says.

Now the grandfather looks up and smiles. With difficulty he pushes himself to his feet. Carrying his guitar by the neck, he shuffles across the square and stands beside the boy. "It's a story for an old man. Not for a boy who has yet to make his future."

The boy stares across the sea. "Sometimes I think there is no future."

"That's because you've been spending too much time in the past with an old man. Me, I'm just a flea on the dog of time now. And the dog is running downhill."

The boy shrugs. "The story took a long time today."

"Did it? I hadn't noticed."

"Maybe I just interrupt too often. I'm sorry."

"It's nothing," the old man says.

He clears his throat. "You should leave here, you know. As your father and brothers did. As Ernesto and Luis will do any day now."

"Where else would be different? It's all the same, isn't it? It's all Mundomuerto now."

"Go into the jungle then. You can always find work in the ruins."

The boy merely shakes his head.

"The city then. There are cities all over the world these days. You'll never know what they're like until you visit a few. Maybe things are different there."

"But in the city," the boy says, "I wouldn't have my grandfather."

"Muchacho," the old man answers, and releases a heavy breath, "if you were my real grandson, I might agree. But I am nobody's grandfather. I fathered nothing but dreams, and all of them were stillborn."

The old man lays a hand on the back of the boy's neck. He leans forward and kisses the boy's hair. The boy cannot bear to turn to him. A moment later the old man shuffles away, out of the square.

"Can I help you this time?" the boy calls after him.

"Gracias, no." And he continues on.

At the end of the street, when the old man reaches the cliff path and turns toward the sea, the boy calls out again. "Yesterday I followed the shoreline for half the morning. And I found no waterfall or meadow. No cabin in need of a roof."

The old man neither pauses nor looks back. He must keep his eyes on the ground now as he descends the path. "If you walk far enough, you will find it."

"And what if I do? What then?"

"It is better to be the head of a sardine, nieto, than the ass of a whale." A minute later the old man disappears from view below the cliff's edge.

The path is a treacherous one, not the same path he used to bound up and down so effortlessly just one short lifetime ago. He uses his guitar as a cane now, it plays the music of steadiness, but even that song has fallen out of tune. It takes him a long time to make his way down to the beach, and another long time across the slippery rocks and into the shallow water where Lucia Luna sits atop the ancient boulder, gazing out to sea.

At times when the boy looks down on them like this, she seems an ugly vulture to him, rapacious thief of the old man's life. At other times, when as now the grandfather touches her lightly on the shoulder and she turns to him with eyes full of bewilderment, glistening with doubt, maybe even void of recognition, at these times the innocence of her confusion makes her young again, and the tenderness with which the old man helps her down off the rock sets soft music to playing in the distance, the music of fiesta riding in on ocean spray, a sigh from the past searching for someone to listen.

The boy watches them struggling onto shore, every step an ordeal, and he wonders what to do. The old man is right, he should leave this place, but where is there to go? And with the boy gone, who would care for the grandfather when he is too old to sweep his own floor or pull on his pants? Who will find shoes for him to wear? Who will listen without laughter to his story?

And when the old man himself fades away, who will hold onto his ghost for him? Who will grasp it tightly when the wind howls, and who will keep the silky thing from being blown into the sea?

The boy knows he can depend on no one else to do what must be done. At fiesta these days, nobody but he ever wonders if a dolphin-man will come ashore to dance with the prettiest girls. The prettiest girls do not remain in Mundomuerto long. And the talk here is not of wild magic but of the machine of life and how to keep the timepiece ticking. People talk desultorily of motors for the fishing boats, of fish with tumors, of rain that kills the trees. No one has seen a jaguar in Mundomuerto for a very long time now. And no one is sad to not see one, except perhaps for Lucia Luna and the old man, and certainly the boy.

The boy watches the two old ones trudging up the path, and he wonders what to do. Off to his right somebody has turned on a radio—the music is loud and hurts his ears. He prefers the softer music that blows in off the water, the delicate chords that accompany the grandfather as he pauses now to pluck a tiny yellow flower from the side of the path. Lucia Luna stands unmoving beside him, always facing the sea, her black rags fluttering. She does not watch the old man as he draws a length of string from his pocket and twists the flower stem around it. He then picks another buttercup, and another, his thick fingers working patiently until he has fashioned them into a bracelet, which he slips over her crepe-skinned wrist. Then the old man reclaims his guitar, and he takes Lucia by the hand, and he escorts her up the path.

At fiesta these days, on Saturday nights when the men come roaring back into town in their pickup trucks, returning from Nuevas Alijas or elsewhere, sore and exhausted and with half their week's pay sloshing around in their bellies, when a plastic boombox is set on the plaza's stone wall and soon everyone is shouting and stumbling against one another in their frenetic and graceless dance, the boy slips away in the darkness and follows a different music down to the beach. The vieja is there, and the old man too, sitting together on a great black boulder of silence. The boy peers into the grandfather's eyes and he sees Lucia Luna's white dress billowing—madre de dios, what a beauty! And together they listen for the splash of a dolphin in the star-speckled vastness beyond.

Lucia Luna eats and drinks nothing but sea air as she waits and waits for her lover's return. The old man vows to defy death another hundred years if necessary, sipping only on the tart nectar of memory's flower. As for the boy, until he grows beyond it he is content to be sustained on hard work and wonder, and on the hope that this world of ours is not truly what it seems.

Photo Credit: Jack Hetrick

Randall Silvis is the author of nine critically acclaimed books, including seven novels, a story collection, and a nonfiction narrative, as well as numerous plays and screenplays. His work has been nominated for the Pushcart Prize and the Frankfurt Book Award and was a finalist for the Hammet Award for Literary Excellence. He is a winner of two NEA fellowships and the prestigious Drue Heinz Literature Prize.